GIVING ALL MY *Love* TO A BROOKLYN *Street King*

Azryah & Kaylen's Love Saga

A NOVEL BY

MISS JENESEQUA

"Don't Ever Play Yourself.

Major Key."

– DJ Khaled

CHAPTER 1

~ *Kaylen* ~

But I didn't cum Kay.

I stared down at the text message before kissing my teeth. Was this bitch serious right now? After all the trouble she had caused me, from the second I had picked her ass up from that night club, I just wanted to have a regular ass night with my niggas, with no stress, no drama.

However, when I laid eyes on shorty, I was hooked. Maybe it was because of that gorgeous face of hers and that banging body to match. I was an ass man, and she had one that was completely out of this world. Seeing her groove and shake it on the dance floor at the nightclub I was at, captivated me completely.

Well excuse the fuck outta me... We both ain't pay for dinner so we both don't need to cum, I texted her back with no remorse. Fuck she thought this was?

Her response rapidly came back. *Kay! I told you I wanted to get to know you better.*

Kaylen: And you knew I just wanted to fuck. Don't act dumb now.

+917 991 6827: *Okay I knew that… But you treated me like shit last night. I thought you wanted me?*

Kaylen: I did before you got into that altercation at Benihanas.

+917 991 6827: *That bitch was all over you though! We were on a date and getting to know each other, but there she was giving you all types of eye contact and you were just eyeing her back.*

Kaylen: Shorty, we were on a date correct. Getting to know each other, again correct. But who the fuck said we were in relationship? I only just met you and you already gettin' your ass worked up, putting hands on the chick that didn't even do nothing.

Kaylen: Now if I fucked her in front of you then I woulda understood your reasons for getting mad.

+917 991 6827: *Okay… I apologize for getting out of character. That's not usually like me. I'm just protective over mine. I would really like for us to try again though.*

Kaylen: Nah, I'm cool.

Kaylen: Lose my number.

+917 991 6827: *Nigga, what the hell?*

Kaylen: I'm pretty sure your ass ain't blind. Lose my fuckin' number or I'll make you lose my fuckin' number. I know where your ass live, remember? Fuckin' try me.

Kaylen: Your number ain't even saved in my phone and you over here acting like some queen. Don't contact me again.

After that, she didn't bother replying, and I could only smile happily at the fact that she had gotten the message. She was going to leave me alone and that's all I wanted. I knew having sex after I had been on an unintentional break away from pussy was going to backfire on me. And it most certainly had. So I was going back on my break and staying away from pussy.

This break of mine wasn't intentional at all. I didn't even know why I had started it. Actually... I knew exactly why I had started it. And every Friday night that I went to New York's hottest strip club to see that one girl perform, only constantly reminded me of my damn sex break. How the hell was I going to get her out of my head? And to make matters worse, guess what day it was today?

Fuckin' Friday.

~ Azryah ~

From the second that I laid eyes on him, while I was on that stage, I knew that he was exactly who I wanted. The fact that he was here right now was everything to me. And I knew that I was going to put on an extra good show tonight, especially because he was front row with his crew. Club Onyx was fully packed tonight, and I knew it was because of me. Who else would all these people be here to see? Those dancers didn't have shit on me. Despite the fact that I hadn't even been working here that long, they still were all shit compared to me. I wasn't even a professional, but here I was, showing these females who claimed that they were the "baddest", how things were done.

"Yo, you see that ass?" I peeped one of his friends mouth to him.

He simply nodded and continued to watch me dance in front of him. I had purposely chosen an outfit tonight that did a shit job of concealing anything. This wasn't my natural element because usually, I had on a bikini that covered up at least my nipples. But I was doing things much differently tonight. I was practically topless in a mesh see-through bikini top and a white G-string.

I was doing things much differently tonight for Kaylen.

Mr. Kaylen Walker. Kaylen. The only man that I wanted attention from tonight. He had a cute, young face, with light mocha, clear skin. On his head, he sported light curls a small beard. Those perfect pink lips were sculpted nicely, and a thin goatee traced around them. He had tattoos right up to his neck, which added extremely to his dangerous, yet sexy persona. Not only was he fine, but he was also very popular too.

A man so confident and suave that I almost wanted to bow down to him. He was the epitome of beautiful. You would rarely hear men be called beautiful, but this man, my God, was beautiful.

Trust me when I say that I was not the only female checking for him tonight. Many others, not just strippers, but attendees of the club, were breaking their damn necks trying to grab his attention. But those brown eyes were only on me.

Back to my dancing though. Like I said, I wasn't a professional, but I could make any man in here think otherwise. As I grinded my hips sexually against the silver pole hanging from the ceiling to the floor, Kaylen's hand was stroking on his goatee. His lips slightly parted, revealing his pink tongue that he used to seductively wet his bottom lip. All while still staring at me.

My bitch is bad and boujee

Cookin' up dope with an Uzi

My niggas is savage, ruthless

We got 30's and 100 rounds too

My hips continued to grind in sync to the upbeat Migos "Bad and Boujee" track before I used my legs to hang off the pole and twirl on it. Within an instant, I had lifted myself upside down and began to spin wildly on the pole, earning a sudden gush of money on me and the red stage below me.

"Damn, yo! She bad, for real," one of Kaylen's boys yelled in excitement.

All I could do was smirk and continue to twirl, spin, and climb on the pole, only adding to the amazement and enthusiasm of the club already. I continued to dance with passion, even though this wasn't my passion one bit. The money was good, yeah, but that didn't mean I loved the job.

Within a few minutes, the music began to fade and I knew that my time was up. I ended with a final split in front of Kaylen and his crew, smiling proudly at them all and throwing in a few winks. Kaylen's handsome face remained emotionless, but I could still see that twinkle of lust in those eyes.

He wanted me.

***

One thing that I hated with all my heart about Club Onyx, was all the unwanted male attention it brought when I wasn't on stage. Like damn, I'm no longer dancing and no longer looking for you to bring out that green. We don't need to have a conversation, nigga; the show is over. Bye bye. Why was that so hard to comprehend for some? It's like niggas loved causing headaches and just causing unnecessary problems.

"Yo, ma, let me holla at you real quick," one boy shouted from his car as I walked through the outdoor parking lot. "Yo, ma! Where you goin'? Let a nigga get those digits though."

The same nigga that was trying to get my attention, was the same nigga that had been staring hard while I had been on stage. Staring hard, with a thirsty look on his face, all while sitting next to Kaylen. I had noticed him from the second I exited Club Onyx. He wasn't ugly, but he wasn't cute either. A brown-skinned dude with big brown eyes, a medium-sized nose, and large darkened lips. Like I said, wasn't ugly, wasn't cute, but most definitely wasn't my type.

"Ma! You were looking real good tonight on that stage... You don't wanna talk to me? Fuck you then, you ugly anyways!" Niggas were truly crazy beings.

Once I made it to my black Lexus, I sighed in relief at the fact that I was now in the one thing that would be taking me straight home. At least now, I could get in my car and not worry about being stalked or called upon annoyingly. Getting into my car and sitting comfortably in my driver's seat, I rested my forehead against my leather steering wheel. A soft sigh left my lips as I contemplated on the warm bath I would be taking when I arrived home. A warm bath and a glass of wine was what I needed. Make that a large glass of wine.

Tap! Tap! Tap!

I rolled my eyes at the sound of light tapping on my window. At first, it had caught me by surprise, but then I remembered the persistent male trying to gain my attention before I had entered my car. I was really going to cuss his ass out if he was going to be consistently desperate and just thirsty. However, as I lifted my head and looked out my car window, my heart almost stopped.

"Open up," he mouthed, throwing me a sexy smirk. I had a strong feeling that he knew how surprised I was to see him. It was written all over my face.

Kaylen Walker, standing outside my car window, tapping on it in order to get my undivided attention. Was this really happening right now? I lightly exhaled before I started my car engine, hoping that he didn't get offended, but I really wasn't about to step out of my car. I was way too comfortable inside already. Once my car engine was on, I watched as Kaylen's face softened from a stern look to a more pleased one, when my car window was all the way down.

"Oh, so you can't get out your car for a nigga?" he asked in a tone that I wasn't sure was supposed to be rudeness or amusement. His hands now rested against my car and had me feeling some type of way, I wasn't sure I understood.

"It's kinda chilly tonight," I responded coolly. "Besides, I hardly know your ass. You could be a stranger in the night sent to kill my ass."

He suddenly laughed in a way that made my insides melt slightly. *What the fuck... even his laugh was sexy.* "A stranger that comes to watch your ass dance every Friday night."

That, he was right about. For the past two months, he had been coming to Club Onyx to see me. That I was sure of. And he always made sure that he left the biggest tips. Him and his crew of fools. I simply shot him a small smile, wondering what he really wanted from me. There was no way he had just come up to my window to make small talk.

"So, can I help you with something?"

"Do you think you can help me with something?"

His question was confusing. It didn't help that his sexy voice made everything sound like rainbows and unicorns in my ears, and seeing his attractive face made me want to risk it all for him tonight. But there was nothing that I required of him tonight.

"No," I quietly answered.

"Are you sure?"

His question sounded taunting. What did he expect me to say to him?

"Are you sure?" I fired back at him. "You're the one asking all the questions. What exactly do you want?"

"You're right about me askin' all the questions," he stated. "If I told you I want you in my bed tonight, what would you say?"

"That you're a crazy ass nigga."

Pause.

I may have been putting a show on for Kaylen earlier at Onyx, but that's all it had been. A show. He wasn't entitled to anything else outside of Club Onyx... for now. I really didn't care how fine this dude was. He wasn't about to think that because I was a stripper, he could get in easy with me. It most definitely didn't work like that.

"Oh, word?" he asked smugly. "Me wanting you naked in my bed tonight, screaming my name, makes me a crazy ass nigga?"

"Si," (Yes) I replied, beginning to roll my car window back up. Kaylen's hands that had been resting against my open window, quickly snatched away. Honestly, he was going to have to try a lot harder if he wanted a piece of me.

"Oh, so it's like that, huh? A'ight, Azryah. Guess I'ma just see your pretty ass around," he concluded just before my car window shut him out.

As I stared into those mesmerizing brown eyes of his, I was even more surprised than I had been when he originally arrived. How the hell did he know my name?

***

"Michelle, are you serious? I've been at work from 5:00pm 'til 1:00am, and you couldn't wash a single dish? But you're up watching *Real Housewives*? Are you fucking serious right now?"

"I'll wash them tomorrow! Get off my damn case. I'm about to sleep."

Michelle Moore. My wonderful roommate aka my best friend. 'Til this day, I was genuinely confused on our friendship. She's lazy as fuck, rude as fuck, and for someone as broke as her, bourgeois as hell. We were best friends, yeah, but we had serious boundaries. We might have been living together, but that didn't make us family. Hell no.

We had rented out a two-floor condo in Brooklyn. She had the ground floor and I had the top. The only things we shared was the kitchen and living room on her floor downstairs. Right now, Michelle had me tight. I had left this house at 5:00pm, making her promise to wash all the dirty dishes in the sink that SHE had used up. How was I telling a grown ass, twenty-five-year-old female to do shit she was already supposed to be doing? Who the hell was I, her damn nanny?

"Michelle, you really not about to do this right now! You know damn well you were supposed to clean your shit."

"I forgot."

This bitch was off work for a week but had somehow forgotten to clean her shit. I was living with a true pig. Best believe, Michelle and I worked at the same place. Club Onyx. Only thing was, she wasn't a dancer, she was a waitress. She had mild scoliosis that had been

10

corrected when she was a kid. But the correction had involved surgery, leaving a long scar down the middle of her back. A scar that she had been too scared to get a tattoo over. That's why she had never had the real balls to strip. However, if it wasn't for Michelle putting in a good word with the owner of Onyx, Lorenzo - I wouldn't have gotten that job. So I guess I owed her that much appreciation. But not that much appreciation that her whole dirtiness and laziness could be dismissed.

"Michelle, you better wash all these damn plates tomorrow, or you're getting whooped. You know I can beat your ass," I yelled to her seriously.

"You can't!" she fumed back. Clearly, she was delusional.

"I can! Don't fuck with me now, girl, unless you want me to give you a few bruises before you go to sleep."

She kept silent after that, and I was grateful that I had won that argument. She was washing all those dishes tomorrow morning, or she would feel my wrath. No doubt about it.

CHAPTER 2.

~ *Azryah* ~

10:40 p.m.

The only thing that had put me in a good mood this whole entire day, was the fact that Michelle had washed every single dish as I wanted her to. That was the only thing keeping me happy right now because having to work the stage tonight was depressing. Why don't I just quit, you ask? I asked myself that question every single day. I really did. But I couldn't quit now. Not now that I've worked so hard to get here. I refused to give up just because things seemed depressing.

I had an hour left to myself until I was up on stage tonight. And right now, I was cherishing everything about spending some alone time. Even if that meant locking myself up in a restroom cubicle. Sometimes, the restroom was the only sanctuary I could really have to myself. Especially because all the dressing rooms for strippers were always noisy, messy, and packed full.

I didn't want to be around anyone else but myself. That's just the way shit was. Yeah, I was antisocial, and I didn't really give a fuck what anyone else had to say. Of course, I had strippers that gossiped about me, or as I like to call them, my beloved haters. My haters were basically a bunch of girls that were salty over the fact that I earned the highest out of every dancer at Club Onyx. They were also salty at the fact that Kaylen Walker came checking for me every Friday night, and not for them. Because of all that, they just constantly stayed talking shit about me. Talking shit wasn't about to stop me from making my moola though, was it? That's why I paid them no mind and decided on focusing on me, myself, and I. That's all I had in the end.

~ Two Hours Later ~

My job was done for the night and I could finally get in my Lexus and head home in peace. But heading home in peace seemed nearly impossible, seeing him resting against my car trunk. Casually resting against my property as if it belonged to him.

"I hope this isn't going to become a habit," I stated as I slowly walked up to him with a look of disapproval.

"And if it does?"

I couldn't deny how good he appeared to me. He was dressed in all black. With black Timberlands on his feet, two silver chains peeking from under his jumper, a stud in each ear, and a small silver nose stud in his nose. A stud I had never noticed before. It had to be new.

"Then I might need to file a restraining order against you."

He instantly laughed at my words. Again, that sexy laugh of his had my insides melting. He needed to get rid of that laugh.

"You wouldn't, yo."

"Oh, I would, yo," I promised, taunting him with a hand on my hips. "Especially since you know my name."

How he had found it out, I had no idea.

"A little birdie told me."

"What birdie?"

He shot me a goofy grin before replying, "A little birdie that I swore secrecy to."

I couldn't help but scoff. What a bunch of absolute bullshit.

"But let's not front here, like I'm the only one who knows names, nigga."

"Your name isn't anything special," I reminded him. "Everyone at Club Onyx knows who you are."

"And who am I?" he cockily asked, making me suddenly roll my eyes with irritation.

"Someone who needs to get the hell off my car."

He gave me a less goofy grin and a grin that had a more devilish appeal. Then he ran his fingers across his goatee in the sexiest way, that made me almost cream in my panties.

"Not until you agree on lettin' me take you out."

"What?"

I was truly astonished now. Was this the same guy that had been watching me perform every Friday night with lustful eyes? The same guy that had told me yesterday that he wanted me naked in his bed, was now asking me out? On a real date? What had the world suddenly turned into? Come to think about the whole situation, Kaylen was never at Club Onyx on a Saturday. He only came on Fridays with his crew, and right now, not a single one of his followers were in sight.

"Well? What do y—"

"No."

His eyes widened with shock.

"Excuse me?"

"I'm pretty sure you ain't deaf," I snapped, knowing I was playing myself right now.

I had wanted this man from the second I laid eyes on him. But I couldn't be one of those easy chicks for him. He couldn't just think that he could win me over with one date and that would be it.

No way.

"I ain't deaf," he fumed. "I'm just tryna make sure you ain't buggin' right now on some bullshit by saying no to me."

"Awwww," I cooed in a fake sweet voice with friendly eyes. "Did I hurt Kaylen's teeny weeny feelings?"

"Yo, don't mock me, nigga."

"Boohoo, go cry me and fuckin' river," I commented sinisterly. "Get off my car, Kaylen."

"Are you really saying no to me right now?" he questioned in disbelief. "I just asked you out on a date! Not for sex, Azryah. On a fuckin' date."

"Go take your mother on a date," I fired back at him.

"She's dead."

Shit.

Now I felt guilty as a motherfucka, trying to come across rude but only to have it backfire on me.

"... Alright. Well, I'm sorry for your lo..."

And that's when I clocked the cheeky smile growing upon his pink lips. This nigga was an absolute liar!

"Get the fuck off my car, asshole."

"Make me."

Saying shit like that was only making his appeal to me grow further. He was honestly starting some shit that I didn't think I was gonna be able to remain calm for. I kept silent but threw him deadly looks with my eyes.

"Make me get off your car, Azryah," he playfully announced.

"It won't take me long to call an Uber to take me home," I informed him simply. "These childish games you're playing are only gonna backfire on you, homie."

"Homie?" he asked with a confused expression. "You and I both know I ain't tryna be your homie."

"You're right," I agreed with him. "We're not homies. We're not anything. So please, just get off my car."

"So, you won't let me take you out, nigga?"

He constantly called me nigga and expected me to show any sort of respect towards him. Wow. He was lucky he was good looking. Ugly niggas could never try this shit with me and think it could slide.

"No, *nigga*..." My words trailed off as I began to muster the biggest lie of the century. One that would definitely get him off my case. "I have a man."

"Did I fuckin' ask for that bullshit?" he rudely queried. "Matter fact, yeah, you do. I'm your man now."

Kaylen Walker was not only aggressive, dominant, and highly annoying, he didn't know when to say no and leave a situation alone.

"Kaylen, you need to get off my car. The answer is no. You are not taking me out on a date, so let it go. And leave me alone," I concluded, sighing deeply. My words were most definitely killing me softly. But the words that had been killing me softly had also managed to get through to Kaylen. I secretly hoped he would stay and challenge me, try to convince me to go on this mysterious date with him. But he didn't.

He simply moved off my car trunk and stepped in front of me. I was slightly intimidated by how tall he was. He had to be over six feet... six feet two? Those brown eyes of his had an emotionless look inside them. A look that made me come to the realization that Kaylen was not going to be as easy to read as I originally believed.

"You're going to regret sayin' no to me, Azryah," he concluded solemnly. His hard gaze locked on my eyes before he finally turned away from me.

***

I sighed deeply before chugging down the remainder of my red wine and listening to Michelle complain for the hundredth time tonight about how she hadn't had some dick.

"I swear I'm about to lose my mind," Michelle ranted.

"It's only been two weeks," I mumbled, embarrassed for myself more than her. I couldn't believe I was listening to her shit right now.

"Two weeks too long!" she yelled. "That's how I know you haven't had some in over a year."

I rolled my eyes before reaching for my phone that set on my lap. It's not like I had anyone texting me, but looking at my phone now would be better than putting up with Michelle.

"I just want some meat back in my life," Michelle exclaimed desperately. "Some big, thick, juicy meat... Is that so hard to ask for? Azryah, is it?"

I shook my head no at her, half listening and more focused on my Twitter timeline. Twitter usually kept me entertained, and it was no different now. A bunch of amusing tweets popped up on my feed and I smirked while retweeting them all.

"You know what... I'm getting some dick!"

I heard her shout, but I had already blocked her out. Once my attention was on something else other than you, it was very difficult to get me to snap out of it. But hearing a loud thud of knees touching the floor and the clasp of hands together made me snap out of it. I looked at Michelle, only to see she was now on her knees, in a praying stance.

What was this girl doing now?

"Dear Lord, I ain't get any dick in a while, so if you wanna throw some my way, I'd appreciate it. Amen," she confidently prayed.

I couldn't believe it. This girl was not only horny as hell, but crazy as hell too. I didn't even know why I was acting surprised, Michelle had most certainly always been a crazy chick back in high school. Chicks knew not to mess with her because she wasn't an easy force. You tried her once, that would be the last time ever you would get the chance to do it. If she wasn't cussing girls out, she was whooping their asses. And when it came to her boyfriends, she convinced all the thirsty girls that she was a Nigerian witch doctor that had a special secret realm with the Nigerian Goddess, Oshun, who could grant her any wish she desired. Including death wishes on girls that didn't understand that her man was taken. Funny thing was, Michelle wasn't even Nigerian. I was. But still, no one dared question her.

"Michelle!" My mouth dropped open as I observed her.

"What?" she asked innocently, getting up from her knees and moving to sit back on the couch next to me. "A girl's gotta do what a girl's gotta do." A smirk formed on her lips before she winked at me.

"I can't stand you, I swear," I told her.

"I love you too," she cooed sweetly, blowing me a kiss.

I couldn't believe I was actually saying this but... The Lord must have answered Michelle's prayers because the following Monday night, a miracle happened.

~ Monday Evening ~

Being a full-time stripper definitely had its cons. The words 'full time' just didn't sit well with me. But again, who was I to complain. I wanted this job and I wanted the money, so I needed to see it out to the end. The very end.

"Krystle, you're wanted in room nine," I heard an order emerge from behind me.

I turned around to see Anna, the manager of all the dancers at Club Onyx. She was in charge of all the strippers and made sure that we all had somewhere to be as soon as we started our shift for the night. Krystle was my stage name that everyone referred to me as. Which is why when Kaylen said my real name, Azryah, I was completely surprised. No one except Anna knew my real name and Michelle of course. But Michelle wouldn't tell him. Anna on the other hand, I wasn't so sure about her.

"Got it," I responded to her coolly before turning back round to see my reflection in the mirror.

Dancers got requested for private room dances all the time, so I wasn't the least concerned. It was all a part of my job. But Kaylen not bothering to request a private dance from me after constantly lusting after me for two months on stage had me baffled. I knew he wanted me, but he just had to work harder. That's all. Then he could have me.

After putting the last finishing touches on my makeup, fixing up my outfit, I was finally ready to go. I headed to room nine, opening up the door and heading inside. The room was pitch black but I lifted my hand towards the light switch and flicked it on.

Then his face appeared making me instantly frown.

"What are you doing here?" I asked him rudely, closing the door behind me and placing a hand on my hips.

"So you don't even greet prop—"

"You shouldn't be here!" I yelled at him, feeling the fury inside of

21

me rapidly grow. "You of all people shouldn't be here, Michael."

"I had to see you," he explained. "To know that you're okay."

"I'm fine," I informed him abruptly. "You need to leave."

"Azry—"

"Michael, please," I desperately pleaded with him. "You need to go."

"I can't," he admitted. "I need to make sure you're safe, that you're okay. You suddenly leave up and out of the blue and expect me not to worry about you. Are you serious?"

All I did was remain silent, not even bothering to respond. I was honestly still confused as to why he was still here. It didn't make any sense to me. The whole thing didn't make sense one bit.

"Okay, Michael, you see that I'm fine, so can you go now?"

His caramel face still appeared so handsome to me after all these months. Those big brown eyes, thick juicy lips, long eyelashes, head full of waves, made him look even better than when I had first seen him.

Meet Michael. My ex-boyfriend.

"Can you please explain to me why you just up and left? Without even saying goodbye? And now you're a stripper? In a whole new state? What the fuck?" he queried in a heartbroken tone.

I knew I had left him heartbroken all those months ago. But a girl had to do what a girl had to do.

"Michael, please..." He just didn't understand how much risk he was putting me into right now. I had to be seen working all the time. I didn't want to get fired.

"I'm not going anywhere," he promised. "Unlike you, I don't just get up and run."

"I never ran, Michael!"

"Yes you did!" he roared, his jaw beginning twitch. "You ran, leaving me." Those big brown eyes of his were beginning to well up with tears.

We had the perfect relationship. Yeah, we had our arguments here and there, but nothing we couldn't live through. He was always so good to me, and we just clicked. We just worked. Seeing him look at me this way had me close to tears too. I never wanted him to see me like this. As a half-naked stripper, unless it was because we were doing a new role play idea in the bedroom, then fuck it. I didn't mind. We had always been one freaky ass couple.

But this wasn't role play. Shit, we weren't even together. So, I was ashamed that he was seeing me like this. However, now wasn't the time to stress about anything other than the fact that Michael was at Club Onyx, when he wasn't supposed to be. I had to get him out, one way or another.

"Michael, you need to leave."

"I'm not going anywhere until you talk to me, Azryah," he sternly voiced.

"This isn't the right place for us to do all of that. Can you just go? You didn't come for a lap dance, you came to ask questions. If my boss watches the CCTV cameras in here and sees that I'm not doing shit but talking to you, I will be fired."

"I just want us to talk. Why are you making this difficult? I haven't seen you in months and this is how you treat me? After all we've been through you just wanna push me to the side."

"Michael…You need to leave."

"I'm not going anywhere, Azryah, until you talk to me."

~ 5 Hours Later ~

After a long day of dancing my behind off for some green, I was grateful and relieved to be home. Away from Michael too. How had I gotten Michael off my case? By giving him my number and promising him that we would talk, only if he backed off for a while and didn't show up randomly at my workplace. That would buy me sometime until I needed to come face to face with him again.

I gracefully walked into the condominium I shared with Michelle, not bothering to stay quiet. It was 1:22am, I knew she was asleep. What the hell would she be doing up at this time when she had work in the morning? But listen to me when I tell you that I was totally wrong. Michelle Moore was not asleep. Ms. Moore was not catching one ounce of sleep.

"Fuck yeah."

Hearing her moans fill my eardrums took me utterly and completely by surprise. Mostly because it had been months since I had heard her moan. Yeah, she definitely hadn't been lying when she said she hadn't gotten it in for two weeks.

"Ugh! Yaaasss, right there, baby!"

Now I was disgusted. Not only was I listening to her moans and the groans of the male company she had, but this shit was getting louder by the second. I needed to head upstairs to my room, lock myself inside, plug my earphones in, and not come out ever again. Minus the not come out ever again apart, I decided to do just that. I headed to my bedroom, locked my door, and fell asleep to the sweet, seductive voice of Amerie.

***

Surprisingly, waking up the next morning wasn't as bad as I thought it would be. One thing I remembered about Michelle's sex habits was that she didn't like having her guests still in her space at breakfast. So by the time she woke up, homie, it was time to go.

Knowing this fact had me no longer feeling disgusted and annoyed by her whole sex escapade. Her sex escapade that probably woke up the damn entire population living on the same condominium floor as us.

I stretched my arms and legs out in my bed, before sitting up and getting out. My silk robe hung on the back of my door and I grabbed it, quickly putting it on before heading out to the kitchen downstairs. All that was on my mind as I headed to the kitchen was the large breakfast that I was going to prepare myself this morning. I had been craving pancakes, eggs, bacon, and sausage for the longest, but just hadn't been bothered to make it. My appetite had cooked up something strong during the night, so I knew that it was going down this morning.

Entering the kitchen, the strong, sweet aroma of pancakes hit my nostrils and I almost had to take a step back. The step back I wanted to take was because of the fact that I knew Michelle wasn't a cook. She preferred having everything done for her, which is why she ordered takeout so much. But maybe she had, had a sudden change of heart.

As I walked in deeper inside, I expected to see Michelle standing by the stove, cooking up our breakfast for the day. Instead of Michelle, I was greeted to a large muscular back of tattoos.

My heart suddenly stopped. Then it continued beating again. Only to beat at a speed that wasn't making any attempts to slow down. Fuck. A large muscular back of tattoos, arm tattoos too - on both arms I might add, that were big too - black sweats cloaking his legs, and Nike sliders on his feet.

What the hell?

But that wasn't even the worst part. The worst part was when that muscular back turned around and I was greeted to those familiar mesmerizing brown eyes.

"What on earth are you doing here?!"

The brown eyes belonged to one man only. I knew them so well because they belonged to the man I couldn't seem to get out my mind.

Kaylen Walker.

"Excuse me?"

"You heard me the first time, nigga. Why you here?"

I didn't understand all the animosity coming from a lady that I had never even laid eyes upon in my entire life. And the disrespectful manner in which she was using to talk to me, wasn't about to be accepted in about three quick seconds.

"I'm here because I was invited by Mi—"

"That's why you were here last night," she snapped, cutting me off.

One.

"But why the hell are you here now?"

"Because Michelle invi—"

"Are you being serious right now? You seduced my best friend into fucking you? That's what we do now?"

Two.

"Well, I don't think that what goes on between Michelle and I is any of your damn bu—"

"You're a fucking dog, Ka—"

Three.

"You better chill on the way you're talking to me, lady," I warned her, taking a step forward, away from the stove and closer to her. "I really don't take disrespect too kindly."

"Kaylen, you must have lost your damn mind if you th—"

"YO!" I yelled at her, making her jump with fear. "I just told you to watch the way you're talking to me. Now you're calling me Kaylen? That's not my name, I'm Khian."

Her pretty milk chocolate face instantly turned white with shock and I watched as her mouth slightly parted open.

"You're not K-Kaylen?" she asked with a nervous stutter.

This is why chicks needed to think more before they decided to speak up. See how much trouble that mouth of yours could land you in?

"No," I sternly replied. "Kaylen's my twin brother. You probably have me mixed up with him."

Then she remained quiet as a mouse, but I wasn't done yet.

"Whatever beef you have with him, that's between the both of you. I really couldn't care less. But don't you ever in your fucking life talk to me in that disrespectful ass way, ever again. I'm not a little boy, I'm a grown ass man. A grown ass man that doesn't hit women, but best believe, I can get a little hood and fuck you up. I'm dead ass serious too."

Still, she remained silent and I was satisfied. She understood how I demanded respect and that's all that mattered. I gave her a blank expression before turning around and tending back to the pancakes, bacon, and eggs, I had been frying. Even though I was no longer staring at her, I could still see her beautiful face and banging body in my mind.

Damn, despite her rudeness, she was most certainly fine. Extremely fine. Curly black hair, brown chinky eyes that housed the longest lashes, a cute long button nose, and milk chocolate skin. A milk chocolate goddess was the name I saw suiting her best.

"Ooooooh, something smells really good up in here," Michelle's voice sounded through the kitchen.

Just as soon as Michelle stepped in, I turned back around to face Mrs. Rude, catching one last glance at her. And those lips... how the hell could I forget about those plump, juicy, kissable li—

"Khi, all this... for me?"

My head turned in the direction of Michelle, who was walking towards me with a loved-up expression. I simply nodded. I don't know why the hell I decided to make breakfast over here. But a nigga was hungry and needed to eat. I thought I could quickly whip up something for myself and then bounce, but apparently, not so. I had been clocked by Michelle's friend and Michelle herself. Now I was stuck.

"Oh, how rude of me," Michelle commented as she grabbed onto my bare torso, wrapped her arms around me, and puckered up her lips. I accepted her quick peck, shot her a weak smile, and watched her turn to her friend. "Azryah, this is Khian... we dated a few months back."

Yeah, we dated, if that's what you wanted to call it. I called it - we fucked and we texted, basically friends with benefits, but Michelle loved to run with her own shit. So I just let her. We reconnected yesterday, when I came down to Club Onyx to chill with my brother, Kaylen.

She had been serving us drinks at the bar and that's when I recognized her. We started talking for a bit, and before I knew it, she was telling me to wait for her shift to be over and then she ended up in the back of my BMW with no panties on. The rest was history. Mrs. Rude simply nodded, not looking impressed, and now avoiding any kind of eye contact with me.

"I'm gonna be in my room if you need me, Mich," she concluded in a low tone.

"No, girl, stay," Michelle insisted. "Khian's made enough for you too."

Really and truly, I had just made enough for three people. Me, myself, and I. I was a big man with an even bigger appetite. I may have been a gym freak but I loved to eat.

"Nah, I don't wanna intru—"

"Stay," I insisted, interrupting her. "I've definitely made enough."

"O-okay," she meekly said, staring at me nervously.

She was probably still in shock at the fact that I had checked her ass for being so disrespectful. She probably hadn't expected me to shoot her down. I guessed that she would think that I was like Kaylen. Kaylen didn't mind a female talking to him crazy, it excited him for some dumb ass reason. But I, on the other hand, hell no. I was a man and I expected to be treated as such. I wasn't a little boy. So what you wasn't going to do was stand there and berate me like some damn child. Unless you wanted to get knocked the fuck out, I suggest you pipe down.

"Khian, this is so good," Michelle complimented my cooking happily, taking slow bites.

"Thanks," I replied sincerely, continuing to get down my food as quickly as I could. It was almost 9:00am, and even though I had a late start at work today, I still wanted to get home ASAP. "What do you think, Azryah?"

Azryah. Yeah, if she's messing with Kay, she sure is in for a wild ride.

"Y-yeah... it's tasty," she stated, still in that nervous tone of hers. And she was still avoiding eye contact with me.

"Good," I concluded before finishing up the last few pieces of bacon I had.

"Khi, are you stay—"

"Nah," I said. "I've got a late start at work, but I gotta get going."

"You want me to see you off, baby?"

Baby?

I knew fucking around with Michelle again was going to be a big mistake. But how could I resist that sweet box of hers? That box that had a nigga going crazy every time he dived into it.

"No," I informed her sternly, before realizing how cold I was coming across. "It's cool, love, I'll see myself out." Then, I leaned across the dining table and planted a soft kiss on her lips. Seeing her gassed smile told me that I had redeemed myself. "I'll hit you up later though."

"You better," she lustfully remarked.

I got up out my seat, picked up my plate, and walked to the sink. Once I had dropped my plate off, I washed my hands, and turned around while drying them on a dry kitchen cloth.

"It was nice meeting you, Azryah."

"...Likewise."

It was certainly an experience meeting Michelle's roommate. A nice one? Nah, but I knew she already knew that. At least I knew now, that if I decided to mess around with Michelle again, I would be greeted by her lovely roommate, Mrs. Rude, in the mornings. Messing around with Michelle again though? That was definitely something that I needed to have a deep contemplation with myself about.

***

"Dr. Walker, a patient in room 201 needs to see you," a nurse informed me with an innocent smile.

"Thank you, Rosalyn. On my way there right now."

Yeah, I was a doctor. Quite a contrast to my twin, the "businessman." But hey, my calling in life had always been helping people. The right way. So studying medicine had always seemed like the right shit to do. And of course, I was intelligent, so I was naturally good at it.

After tending to the patient who needed to see me and making sure that all the patients who needed to be seen had been, I took a quick break in my office. The first thing that caught my eye on my desk was my flashing phone, alerting me of the text messages coming in. I picked up my phone as I sat down in my large, black, rotating chair before beginning to inspect my texts.

I really enjoyed last night handsome. And if you're down for a part two tonight, I'm all yours.

Michelle.

I wasn't surprised she was texting me back so soon. I had the type of shit that chicks went absolutely crazy for. When they laid eyes on what I was packing and how I delivered it, they wanted me forever. That's why

I had to be careful about who I was letting have some of me all the time. And that's why, I never let anyone commit to me. I was my own self-made, independent man and I didn't need no chick slowing me down. I had goals, standards, and shit to get done. No pussy, no matter how bomb it was, was gonna allow me to become distracted.

Yo bro, I need your help with something.

Kaylen.

My wonderful twin brother, Kaylen. I had come out into the world, two minutes before he had, automatically making me the wiser one out of us both. Which is why he was always coming to me for advice, help, etc.

I had always told him I never wanted any parts of his street shit, that was all on him. He was the one that needed to figure that shit out by himself, since he was the one that had decided to get involved in it. But when shit started popping off and things started getting hot, who else was he going to turn to? Certainly not those goons of his. He couldn't trust any of them with his life. It didn't matter if they worked for him and constantly swore loyalty. Any one of them could be a snake and be ready to stab him right in the back, while still swearing loyalty to him forever. They could each be an Iago. Secretly pulling strings behind Kaylen's back to make him fall like Othello.

So that's why I taught him to always be smart and always be alert. Never give too much shit out and always have your eye on yourself. I didn't want any parts of his street shit, but I didn't want his street shit to land him in jail or worse - death. Therefore, I had to be there for him, whenever he needed me.

I quickly typed back, *I got you bro. Meet me at mine once I'm done at work.*

A few quick seconds and he responded.

Bet.

~ *Michael* ~

She had moved to a whole different state and somehow expected me not to find her. We were together for a while and then, she just up and left me. Two years was most definitely a while. She had left me in Chicago and without even a letter explaining why she didn't want to be with me anymore. She just sent a text saying that she was leaving Chicago and not planning to come back any time soon.

I had used my contacts at the FBI to get a hold of her and now, here we were. She was a stripper and I wasn't impressed one bit. I was irritated. It didn't make any sense to me on why she was doing a degrading job, dancing for a group of thirsty ass niggas every night. Even though she had ended things between us, I still loved her. I wanted to be with her again and I was going to make it my mission to get us back together again.

I was staying in Brooklyn for a while anyways, so I could keep my eye on her. There was a new case that I was working on. A case that had something to do with one of the most notorious, sociopathic criminals of Brooklyn.

Kaylen Walker.

I had been transferred from Chicago to come on board to help the current officers on his case. I had a high rate of arresting criminals, drug dealers, and murders of the streets of Chicago and that's why chief offered me a new job in Brooklyn. I was here to bring down Kaylen's entire organization and send him straight to jail. There was no doubt about it.

Kaylen's rude, arrogant twin brother had me tight.

"Where did you meet him?"

I couldn't believe it. No man had ever talked to me in that way before. Just because patriarchy had existed since the beginning of time, didn't mean it existed in my time. Patriarchy may have socialized you into believing that all males ruled the world and dominated, but guess what? In my world, shit was different. Much different. Pussy ruled and females dominated.

You think a man can just tell me what to do, how to act? I act in whatever way I see fit. No man will ever tell me how I need to act. I tell myself how I act and it's all good. Then a fucking man had suddenly come out of nowhere and burst my bubble of matriarchy.

"I had to take my mother to the hospital a few months ago and there he was."

"Hospital? Michelle, what was he doing at the hospital?"

I don't know why I continued to believe that Kaylen was in my kitchen. They looked the same but there was nothing alike about them, except their faces.

"He's a doctor."

A doctor? Wow.

Khian Walker was attractive, I couldn't even front like he wasn't.

With those breathtaking tattoos that sat on his body, his muscular toned body that was a work of art. He had a clean fade cut that sported kinky curls on top of his head, with medium faded sides, with a neatly groomed goatee that extended across his handsome face into a light, full facial beard, those alluring pink lips... Man, I swear, he was a much older, more mature twin version of Kay. Too fine for you not to notice him. I don't even know why I assumed he was Kaylen, when I had clearly noticed that he didn't have tattoos up to his neck and on his hands like Kaylen did.

"What's up with all these questions anyway?" Michelle queried suspiciously. "He's my man, not yours."

"I've never seen him before," I responded quietly, a small sting of jealousy hitting me because of Michelle's words about Khian being "her man."

He didn't look like her man. They just looked like they were fucking and texting. Nothing special. Friends with benefits was what I saw their relationship as.

"That's because I cut him off for a while and when I was messing with him, you weren't living with me yet."

I stared blankly at her, not even bothering to pay attention to her anymore. In a few hours, I would be getting ready to go to work and Khian would hopefully be a distant memory.

"Is he coming around again tonight?" I asked, wanting to know if I needed to start thinking of finding a new place to stay.

"He hasn't texted me back yet so I don't know," she admitted with a sigh, "But there's a possibility he could be."

I simply nodded at her while saying a silent prayer to the Lord above, please don't let Khian text her back. I could really do with some peace and quiet tonight.

~ *Four Nights Later* ~

"Krystle," Anna called me and I already knew what time it was.

"Room nine, I got it," I informed her, fixing my outfit and getting ready to head to the private dancing room.

I already knew that someone had booked me for an hour, but I wasn't aware who. I was just glad to be away from the stage tonight, because the past four nights, I had continuously been dancing my ass off on stage. I was honestly over it. The same way I was over this shit every single week. Upon entering the dark room, I sexily walked in and flicked on the light switch. I was initially excited to dance for a stranger that had gotten me off the stage tonight. But that excitement quickly died down once I laid eyes on him.

"Wow," he stated in pure shock. Good shock of course. "If I'd known that this is how you get ready for private dances, I would have come sooner."

I didn't have the energy to argue tonight. I was tired and quite frankly, not in the mood. So if that's what he had come here for, he could count me out.

"Bye, Kaylen," I concluded tiredly, beginning to turn around to face the same door I had entered through.

"Whoa," he exclaimed. "Don't leave."

"You're messing around," I stared. "This is my place of work. Not somewhere you can continue playing games."

"How am I playin' games, when a nigga paid for your service for one hour?"

I slowly turned back 'round to face him. "So, you really want a dance?"

He nodded sincerely and relaxed back into the red, plush, leather sofa he was sitting on.

"I really want a dance," he announced, finessing his facial hair in that sexy way that drove me wild. "Unless you don't wanna give me one, I'm sure I can find so—"

"No touching. No kissing. No rubbing," I warned him in a strict, nonchalant tone. "I'm the one dancing for you. I do the touching, you just sit back and stay calm."

He gave me a stiff nod, telling me that he understood my words 100%. And so I took a deep breath and counted to five before sauntering towards where he sat. I took another deep sigh when the automatic music system began to play.

You would think it's all mine the way I took it

Drake at this time, really? And not even a fast, quick song of his - more of a slow, seductive one.

You would think it broke down the way I push it

You hate it when I coat things all in sugar

You want to hear the real talk, well, girl, who wouldn't?

I had taken a seat on Kaylen's lap, to start with. And now, I was slowly rotating and grinding my hips to the soft Drake song. As much as I hated giving private dances, they were fun. It let me know that even with just one person and one song, I still had the moves to bring a nigga weak to his knees. Clearly, I was doing something right because it was only a few quick seconds when I felt Kay's big friend poking my butt. I turned around to sneak a peek at his face, only to see his eyes looking straight at me. The lust was evident and him biting his lips told me that he was only wanting me more and more.

Working, working, working, working, ain't ya?

You don't have no time to lay up

You just trying to be somebody

'Fore you say you need somebody

Get all your affairs in order

I won't have affairs, I'm yours, girl

Faithful, faithful, faithful, faithful

When the hook hit, I changed things up drastically. By drastically, I mean things got... interesting. If he thought I was being shy when I had just first started, then he was about to get a shock of his life.

"Damn, Azryah..."

I twerked for him in beat to the song, then I rocked my body against his, pushing myself towards his chest as I grinded directly on his growing bulge in his pants. I rested my head against his shoulder and turned my head to the side to look at him. All while still dirty dancing for him.

"You like that?" I whispered to him sweetly, continuing to dance for him and have him going crazy for me.

He quickly nodded, sneaking a peek down at my breasts that were covered in a thin, red bikini top. I instantly grabbed one of his tatted hands that were resting against the couch and placed it on my right breast.

"I thought you said no touchin'," he announced in a tense voice.

"Rules can be broken," I explained gently, rotating my hips against his body in sync to the music.

"They can?"

"Yeah."

I want to get straight to the climax

Have you cumming all summer like a season pass

"So, can we break some more rules?" he queried in a low tone, with his hand that was on my breast, now tightly squeezing on it. I felt a small pool form on my thong.

I want to turn you out like pitch black

Want to watch you do work while I sit back

'Cause you talk like you got what I need

"No, Kaylen," I responded, still concentrating on my dancing. But with the way he had touched me, I was finding it very hard to concentrate.

You talk like you got the juice and the squeeze

Talk like you bet it all on me

You can't take no L's off me

"Why not?" he asked. I could hear the amusement in his voice. Almost like he was laughing at me. "Rules can be broken," he stated, repeating my words from earlier on.

"Kaylen, you ca..." However, my words suddenly trailed off once I felt lips touch my skin.

His soft lips were now kissing seductively on my neck. Then he started sucking tenderly and I swear I almost passed out. And as much as I wanted him to stop, my heart knew I was lying. I needed him to continue. No words could even form in my mouth to tell him to stop, no strength could emerge out of me to push him away. I had become weak to Mr. Kaylen Walker.

I simply closed my eyes and enjoyed his sweet kisses on my body. It all felt so damn good. Especially because his hand that had been squeezing on my breast, was now stroking on it and somehow, his other hand had joined in on the fun. Now both my breasts were being tended to, while I had a seducer making love to my neck. Damn him for being such a good charmer and seducer. Damn him indeed.

"Kaylen... please, oh," I moaned, drunk with lust at the feeling of his large hands squeezing and rubbing tightly on my mounds.

"You like that, huh?" his deep voice whispered cockily into my ear as he continued to firmly press his fingers into my breasts. "You like me squeezing on your tits like this, Azryah? See... I figured your sexy ass was a freak deep down."

I didn't like the fact that I had suddenly become weak and fragile to him. I didn't like the way my body was responding to him, telling me that we needed more. I didn't like the fact that his aroma was all around me and I wanted to drown in it. That's how good he smelt. *Fuck*. If I didn't get him to stop now, I was going to be in trouble. But even knowing that I was going to be in trouble wasn't encouraging me to tell him to stop.

No encouragement came when he stopped kissing on my skin and turned my chin towards him. No encouragement came when he pressed his lips against mine. And absolutely no encouragement came when he began to passionately tongue me down. I knew now that we had started something...Trouble.

***

Kissing. An act so simple yet to intimate. Kaylen and I had done a lot of kissing and touching for approximately half an hour. He was a really good kisser as well, which didn't make things any easier for me. And he tasted like everything a man should. Minty and fresh. How the hell was I supposed to resist that? Funny thing was, we had done nothing else but kiss. And when we were completely out of breath, Kaylen said the dumbest shit ever.

"I gotta go."

There he was, straight out of the door without leaving me a number or an address. I was irritated and I didn't understand why. He had been coming to watch me dance at Club Onyx for two months, requested a private dance for an hour, only to use thirty minutes of his time to kiss me. Then the nigga just left?!

Left me horny, wet, and angry. I was completely shocked for words and knew that messing with him had been trouble. Nothing but trouble. Trouble because now, I was back home, in my bed, and with

Kaylen on my mind. He was the only person on my mind. And my frustrations were mounting because all that kissing had left me hot and bothered for him. If he had told me to get naked for him right then and there, I wasn't sure if I would object.

For the first time in years… my dominant personality had lessened and I had let a man control the way I felt about him. What the fuck was going on with me?

CHAPTER 3

~ Kaylen ~

"*You kiss a girl for more than thirty minutes and you're going to end up wifing her, then falling in love with her ass.*"

"*What the...Kaylen, you must be crazy. That shit ain't true.*"

"*It sure is.*"

"*Who the hell told you that?*"

"*Nobody, I just know it's true, man.*"

I had told my boy, Lionel, the fact of kissing girls for more than thirty minutes, fully believing that shit. Only to now, not want to believe in it at all. Because if it was really true, as I had said it was three years ago, I was now in trouble. Big ass trouble.

As I lay casually on my California, king-sized bed, I contemplated about the fact that I couldn't get this chick out my head. It obviously didn't help that she was fine as hell. She had chocolate skin, a gorgeous face, and an absolutely banging body to match. How the hell was I supposed to resist that? It's like God had created her for me, knowing that I would absolutely go crazy once laying eyes on her. And that's exactly what had happened. One look at her and I was now sprung. I didn't want to look any females except her. See what the fuck she had started?

The funny thing was, I really wasn't about to chase her. Or so I thought. I didn't like to chase pussy. You either gave it to me or you didn't, I didn't care. There were plenty other girls that I could bag. See that's the mentality I had originally had when Azryah had first rejected me, but that mentality had gone straight out the window when I started having dreams about her.

Dreams about how amazing it would be for me to slide right up in that pussy and give her the shit that could loosen up her bad ass attitude. Dreams about how good it would feel gripping onto that waist, while I had her pinned against my wall, with absolutely nowhere to run, while I dicked her down and shut that smart-ass mouth of hers up. Yeah, I couldn't sleep after the first one started. But when I kept on having dreams about her, I decided to just let nature take its course and beat my dick while I thought about her.

So now, I couldn't get her out my head and it was only a few days after her rejection, and all the wet dreams that I decided I had to have her. Having her meant that I needed to chase her. And needing to chase her, led to me paying for her services for one hour, only for it to lead to me tonguing her down for more than thirty minutes.

Now, I was pissed. Kaylen Walker didn't fall in love. For all good reasons, too. It was a trap designed to make males, like myself, fail. I wasn't wifing no chick and I sure as hell wasn't going to fall in love with her. But for some odd reason, while kissing Azryah, I realized I didn't even want to smash her yet. I wanted to get to know before I had her. I wanted to know her interests, her dislikes, her hobbies and anything else there was to know about her. Then I could have her in my bed with no panties on.

Crazy shit, right?

I didn't know what was going on with me because this wasn't my usual behavior. Like I said before, I didn't chase chicks. They basically chased me! I'm not an old-fashioned type of dude either, call it new fashioned. I get what I want, when I want it and even when I don't get what I want the first time, there's always an alternative the second time.

I didn't know what the hell I was gonna do about this Azryah chick though. Do I do all this chasing, then smash and leave? Or do I actually take the time to get to know her, still smash and instead of leaving, possibly stay? I blamed the fact that she was a chocolate goddess on why I wanted her so bad.

A milk chocolate goddess with skin so smooth and perfect that I badly wanted to run my fingers across her naked body at night. I wanted to rub her smooth skin down with some coconut oil, kiss every part of her body, down to her thighs. Before opening them up and diving straight into that pu—

What the actual fuck?

I hardly knew this chick at all and I was lusting over her ass. What was wrong with me today? You would think after how rude she was to me, I would be turned off. But I wasn't. Matter fact, the shit made my dick hard, but still pissed me off at the same damn time. And that kiss. God, what was I going to do about her?

Man, I didn't know... but what I did know was that I needed to talk to someone about this shit. And there was only one person I wanted to air out all my problems to.

***

"So, you kissed her?"

I sighed deeply before nodding my head in response to my brother's question. It didn't help that I had been thinking about the shit that went down last night non-stop. I just couldn't get Azryah out of my head.

"Did you want the kissing to lead to something or...?"

"Yeah, bro, of course," I responded calmly. "I thought I was gonna smash her right then and there, but I realized I didn't want to stop kissing her. Now I want to keep kissing her ass. Matter fact, she's the only woman apart from Serayah, I've ever kissed like that."

"Dead ass?" The shocked tone in Khian's voice was evident. Serayah had been my high school sweetheart from over a decade ago. So it was shocking to Khian that I hadn't experienced the emotions I felt with her with any other girl.

"Dead ass serious, bro," I explained with another sigh. "You know I don't kiss bitches man, that shit's a curse. Kiss a girl for more than half an hour an—"

He finished off my sentence for me, "And you gon' end up wifing her ass, I know, I know." He then grabbed his glass of vodka and coke, and took a large gulp before placing it back down on the kitchen counter. "This is probably just lust for you though, Kay. We both know you're not one to fall quickly for chicks."

"Exactly," I replied. "That's what I thought when I first made my move on her. And she's a stripper? When have I ever fallen for a stripper?"

"Are you going to keep on chasing her or leave her alone? 'Cause the only thing I see at this point is if you keep trying to pursue her, you'll end up in a relationship with her."

"I don't want a relationship though," I stated. "Well... I don't think I do."

"You haven't even been in a serious relationship since, shit I don't even know. Since high school. This could work for you. I've already told your dumb ass that you can't be a single hoe forever."

I frowned at his choice of words. He knew how much I hated him calling me a hoe, but the nigga did it anyway. It didn't help that he was older than me by two minutes. Because of that, he felt like he was above me and wiser. But who was the one making real hustler moves, while he sat in a hospital day doing boring shit? Looking after people had always been Khian's calling, I guess, whereas mine had always been about getting that green.

"Firstly, I ain't a hoe, so cut that shit out," I snapped at him, reaching for my Hennessey on the marble counter in front of me.

"Oh, so what are you then?" Khian curiously queried with an arched brow. "You go around fucking whichever bitches can have you, and you claim you're not a hoe?"

I hadn't actually fucked anyone else for a while now, except that chick I had messed around with last week. But she didn't even count because she was whack and brought drama. So, a whole month, in fact,

51

I had gone without having some decent sex. It definitely had something to do with the fact that I was seeing a half-naked Azryah on stage every Friday night, deeply dissatisfied with the fact that she wasn't going to be in my bed at the end of the night.

The reason why I hadn't made a move on her sooner was because I wanted to see if she was one of those strippers that fucked around with anyone or anybody. I let a few of my boys try and get her digits or better still, take her home for the night. But not a single one of them had succeeded.

That only let me know that she was someone who I could smash with no deep regret. She wasn't a hoe but her stripping at Club Onyx made her seem like one. Not that I had anything against strippers, I mean go ahead and get your money, girl, but I'll be damned if the girl I get married to turned out to be a stripper.

"I haven't had sex in a while… The last chick I banged don't even count 'cause you know I'm all for makin' sure both of us get a nut. I ain't even let her ass moan too loud," I informed Khian in a sad tone. "'Cause all I keep thinking about is this girl."

"I think if you want her, you should go ahead and get her."

For the first time ever, Khian was actually on my side when it came to females. Like I said, he was the wiser one out of us, so whenever I told him about my plans to get a chick only for sex, he would instantly shoot me down. Of course, I never listened to him and always did what I wanted. But now, I wasn't even sure if I should listen to him because he was telling me what I wanted to hear.

"What if I fall for her, Khi?" I asked meekly, staring at him in the search for some answers.

"Then you fall for her," he responded in a casual way. "Falling for someone isn't going to kill you, Kay. I don't know why your ass is acting like it will, but it won't."

"But what if it does?"

"Kaylen," Khian lightly laughed. "Just go for her, nigga. You obviously want her if you've been unable to get her off your mind. Like the bullshit you always tell me, you're single. So go do what your single dumb ass wants."

Could I really go ahead and pursue her? Just because she was on my mind, didn't mean I had to follow suit, right? But then, if I didn't follow suit, then things weren't going to be good because she would still be on my mind and I wouldn't have her in my bed. My main fear was having her in my bed once and wanting to see her in my bed over and over again. And then our situation leading into a relationship. Fucking around was one thing, but being in a relationship was a whole other thing.

"What about you?" I questioned Khian, wanting to divert the subject away from me now. I no longer wanted to think about the possibility of having a relationship with Azryah. It was time to move on to my brother's love life.

"Huh?" He shot me a confused look. "What do you mean?"

"I mean, besides your boring ass job, who you messing with?"

"Firstly, being a doctor ain't boring, fool. And secondly... No one."

"Bullshit."

"No one you need to be worried about."

"I knew it!" I exclaimed with a happy smirk. As much as my brother liked to hold this angelic, innocent title because of him being a doctor, he still fucked around from time to time. "Who is she?"

I wasn't surprised anyway. We were identical twins, so we looked exactly the same. If chicks were crazy about me, then chicks were certainly crazy about him. The only difference between us both was the fact that Khian was a gym freak. He had bigger muscles in comparison to me. I was more on the skinner scale 'cause I wasn't a regular gym attendee. But the shit didn't bother me because I had been pulling bitches with the same body for years. So I was Gucci.

"No one you need to be worried about."

"Who said I'm worried?" I asked with a grin, nudging my brother in his arm lightly. "I just wanna know what chick you've got in your sheets. Although, you ain't been messing around with anyone but that waitress from Club Onyx."

Khian remaining silent at my words told me one thing. I had hit the nail on the head.

"It ain't like I ain't messed around with her before," Khian explained. "Besides, she's good in bed, her spot's the perfect place to get busy in but she's crazy. Crazy to the point that she won't let me go."

"What do you mean?"

Khian then reached into his back pocket, brought out his phone, unlocked it, and shoved it in my face. I grabbed the phone and began to read the text messages in front of me.

Michelle: I miss you daddy.

Michelle: When are you coming to see me?

Michelle: A part two is needed of what we did the other night.

Michelle: Call me.

Michelle: Seriously Khi, I miss you.

Michelle: Call me soon?

"Yikes," I said in response to seeing all her messages. "Desperate ain't she?"

"That's not even the best part," Khian voiced in an irritated tone. "She won't stop Snapchatting me."

"Snapchatting you?" I asked in surprise. This nigga had a whole female Snapchatting him and I couldn't even get Azryah to let me take her out when I first asked. "Snapchatting you what?"

"What you think?"

"You gon' let me see?"

"Hell no, nigga, get your own," Khian retorted. "But what I will say is, that body of hers is a problem. Got me almost wantin' to give her my address so I could see it in person again."

I couldn't help but lightly chuckle at his words. This nigga was low-key sprung and didn't even know it yet.

"I don't want her getting the wrong idea though. I'm not trying to get into a relationship with her at all."

"Then you really better let her know that shit," I told him. "Or she'll just keep pestering you until kingdom come."

"Man, I don't know," he answered. "The only reason why I'm really puttin' up with this shit is 'cause her box is bomb."

"And you call me a hoe?"

"You still are," Khian affirmed. "I've only been messing around with Michelle, you mess around with every chick that you lay eyes on, that you like."

"But I could change that."

"By getting with this girl, who you haven't said the name of."

"Azryah."

"Huh?"

"Her name's Azryah," I announced. "Got her real name off her boss. But her stage name is Krystle."

"Oh shit… Azryah? Chocolate chick, nice body?" He questioned me, describing her to me perfectly.

"Yeah, yeah," I replied tensely, afraid about what he was about to reveal to me. I prayed he hadn't fucked her. "How you know her?"

"Nah, not personally, but I met her ass the other day at Michelle's crib."

"Oh word? They're roommates?"

"Exactly, bro, so chill, I ain't fuck her if that's what you're worried 'bout, so fix that face, fool," he noted, beginning to smirk at me.

I loosened up my tense face and lightly chuckled at him, feeling relieved that he hadn't smashed the girl I was after. One thing my twin and I had always made clear to one another was that we were never gonna let a girl come between us. "Aye, I'm cool, fool. So what did you think of her?"

"Can't lie, she's sexy as fuck but that mouth." He paused as he shook his head in disapproval. "A mothafuckin' problem."

That, he was 100% right about. "What'd she say to you?"

"She thought I was you, nigga, started going off on one about me smashing Michelle."

"Oh, so she thought you were me and that I had messed with her roommate?"

"Yup. I had to check her ass too for that, then she was as silent as a mouse," he voiced. "She definitely likes you though. 'Cause the jealousy on her face when she thought I was you... boy, that was something."

All I could do was grin widely at his words. Hearing Azryah become jealous over me was like music to my ears. This only made me want to pursue her even more and get her into my bed. And trust me when I say, she's was going to end up in my bed. It was only a matter of time.

~ *Michelle* ~

Khian not answering my messages or calls had me very frustrated. I wasn't the type to go running for dick because dick usually chased me. That was mostly because of how well I put it down in the bedroom, but for some odd reason, Khian wasn't playing his role right. He had me chasing him around like I was boo boo the fool and him sitting back, watching like I was just his personal entertainment.

I threw my phone in anger to the side of my bed, before closing my eyes and trying to contemplate about why he hadn't texted or called back yet. Maybe I wasn't as good as I thought I was in bed. But surely, if that was the case, he would have blocked my number. He was enjoying me chasing him, I could tell without even needing to see him. He was definitely loving it. And for that reason, I knew I needed to stop.

If he wanted me or not, the decision was no longer his. I was no longer going to stress about a guy that wasn't paying any of my bills or breaking out my back every night. What was the point of that? Yeah, I needed to be done with him. Men were trash anyways.

Wednesday evening had arrived and that meant work. Azryah had driven us both to work tonight and because of that, I had arrived an hour early to my shift. So, I decided to kick it with her in the dressing room that she hated to be in because all the dancers at Club Onyx were all devils in disguise, mostly jealous of her and her success.

I mean, I was a little thrown off when Azryah told me she

wanted to strip. She used to be a childcare worker; you see, and from my perspective, it looked like she absolutely loved that job. But when she called me up one day, begging me to hook her up at Club Onyx, I willingly agreed. I didn't blame her for switching up occupations though. Strippers earned what childcare workers earned in one single week.

"You should really consider getting that tattoo, girl. It would be fun to have a partner on stage," Azryah suggested while fixing herself in the glass mirror in front of her that had white lights around it.

"Hmm, maybe," I lied, knowing fully well I wasn't considering shit. That tattoo just wasn't for me. I didn't like pain at all and I knew that was what getting a tattoo was going to bring, pain. But, I was jealous that Azryah was getting all this moola and extra attention being a stripper. It almost made me want to be her.

"I'm about to go on, so I guess I'll see you outside later on?"

I quickly nodded. "Good luck tonight, not that you need it anyways. You're a born natural." Yeah, she was a natural and that's what I hated the most. Why the hell did she have to be such a good dancer? I low-key hated her for that. Every day, I kept telling myself I was better than her because I wasn't doing a degrading job but deep down, I knew she was better. She was prettier and earning more money.

She shot me a warm smile and watched as I got up out my seat, eyed all the dancers staring at me while having their private conversations, and left the room. I had twenty minutes 'til my shift for the night started so I decided to go ahead and get started. Once dressed in my uniform, I got behind the bar and began serving drinks alongside Sharon.

"Someone's early," she remarked.

"Yeah, my friend got here too early. It's definitely not becoming a regular thing."

"Knowing you, I knew it wasn't gonna be," she commented smugly.

I playfully rolled my eyes at her before turning my eyes to the newest customer at the bar. It was only one look into those brown eyes that I felt my heart stop.

"Can a nigga get a drink from the beautiful server or do he gotta beg for it?"

Shit.

I didn't like that he was just a few meters away from me. One leap over the bar, and I would be next to him, as close as I wanted to be. But that wasn't happening. As much as I was delighted to see him, I was also very annoyed. He couldn't answer any of my messages or calls for the past week since he had fucked my brains out, but here he was at my workplace, without a single care in the world about my feelings.

"Sharon," I called out to my colleague who had her back turned towards the drinks fridge.

"What's up, girl?"

"This young man needs a drink," I stated through gritted teeth before walking towards the bar gate entrance and walking out.

I needed to get far away from him as possible. It didn't matter that he was handsome, I was now convinced that him being that fine was all part of ploy to get me to succumb to him, but absolutely not. It wasn't happening.

"Get yourself together, Mich," I said to myself as I headed to the restrooms.

With the amount of money the owner earned at Club Onyx, you would think he would invest in getting separate staff toilets. But the nigga was stingy with his money, so staff had to use the customer restrooms also. Going to the restrooms allowed me to breathe for a few minutes. I didn't like how bad seeing Khian played with my emotions. It didn't help that he was looking ridiculously fine.

But screw him for showing up at my workplace after ignoring all my messages and calls. I didn't appreciate him suddenly turning up here at my place of work, thinking everything was fine between us because it wasn't. It really wasn't. After looking at my reflection for five minutes and coaching myself on how to get it together, I quickly peed, washed my hands, and decided to head back out there and carry on my shift for the night.

Because I had arrived early, I was also planning on leaving early. There was no way I could stay 'til 1:30am. I made my way towards the restroom door, but the minute I tried to open it, the door was pushed open. I stepped back and watched with half shock and half displeasure at the figure who had now stepped into the restrooms. Female restrooms to be exact. Damn him and his extremely attractive face, those mesmerizing eyes, that body, and don't even get me started on that dick.

"Thought I might find you here."

"Move," I snapped, unable to hide my irritation from him.

"Mich, I only came to see you. What's up with all this resentment?"

I couldn't help but scoff as I looked up at him. After ignoring me for days, he had the audacity to ask why was I angry. Had he gone mad all of a sudden?

"Move."

I didn't want to hear anything he had to say. It was all going to be rubbish as far as I was concerned. Absolute trash, just like him. Yeah, he had now turned me into one of those 'all men are trash' women.

"Michelle, baby girl..."

"Move out of my way, Khian."

He knew how much him calling me baby girl influenced me. It made me weak and fall for his charm all the time. But today, time had changed. I was done with his bullshit.

"I just wanna talk," he explained, pushing his hands deep into his pockets.

"You've been talking for the past five minutes. Just get the fuck outta my way, I need to work."

"Michelle, I—"

"Move!" I yelled at him furiously, my chest now heaving up and down. "Get out of my wa—" *Click!*

The sound of the restroom door being locked filled my ears and seeing that Khian had taken one swift motion to do it, caught me off guard slightly. But what caught me completely off guard was when Khian stepped away from the door and moved towards me.

"All I wanted to do was talk," he announced in a low, tense tone, while still moving towards me. I, on the other hand, was stepping further away from him into the restroom. "But I see talkin' ain't gonna work 'cause of that smart-ass mouth of yours."

He had a look I knew all too well plastered upon his handsome face right now. A look that told me he was tired of trying to use words to get me to hear him out. A look that I had seen many times before, when he had me pinned in one spot and all six inches off him deep in my guts.

"I don't wanna talk or have anything to do with you, Khian," I affirmed, still backing away from him and scared that soon, I would have no other space to back away into. Soon, I would reach one of the restroom walls and I would be trapped. "I'm done talking to you! You ignore my texts and calls and waltz up in here like it's fine."

"A nigga been busy, Mich," he explained wholeheartedly. "You know this."

"Bullshit," I spat before raising a hand in the hopes of getting him to stop coming closer. "Just leave me alone, Khian, clearly you don't want me. I'm not the girl for you." Me raising a hand, did nothing because he still continued to move closer to me.

"If I didn't want you, would I be here right now?" he queried with an arched brow.

"I don't know and I don't ca—" *Thud!*

The sound of my back hitting hard against the restroom wall sounded, and I felt my face fall in defeat. I was now officially trapped in Khian's presence.

"You don't care that I want you?" he asked, walking his last few steps, until he was standing directly in front of me.

I figured that the best thing for me would be to ignore anything he had to say. Maybe he would see that as a message to leave me alone.

"Michelle."

I kept silent, my head facing the floor so I was able to avoid eye contact with him.

"Answer me," he ordered firmly, grabbing my chin, making me look up at him. Those brown eyes were filled with annoyance but also lust.

"No," I rudely responded. He wasn't the boss of me. But my whole 'he wasn't the boss of me' quickly backfired when Khian pressed his body up against me, closer than before.

"No, what?" he questioned in a sexy whisper as he glared down at me.

Shit.

What was he doing to me?

It didn't matter how hard I tried to fight my feelings for this guy, they just always loved to make an appearance. And with how close he was to me, I was becoming wetter and wetter by the second. The smell of his seductive cologne filled my nostrils and I swear I was becoming high. And his hand that had been at the end of my chin, had now slid down my jawline and was now slowly wrapping around my throat. Fuck, he had turned me on before I had even had to chance to realize what the hell was going on.

"No..." What were we even talking about? I swear the subject had flown straight out of my head.

"No, you don't care how hard my dick is right now 'cause of you?"

Shit.

All I could do was softly sigh and keep a locked gaze up into his brown eyes.

"No, you don't care how bad I want to rip all that shit you got on, hidin' that body of yours from me?"

Each question was just driving me more and more crazy for him, for his touch, for his kisses and most importantly, for his dick.

"No, you don't want me to fuck you on that counter right now?"

"Khian," I quietly called out his name.

"No," he affirmed, slightly tightening his hand around my neck. "Answer me."

I couldn't deny it anymore. It didn't matter how pissed I had been with him a few minutes ago. He had me all hot and bothered for him now, not to forget, wet. I needed to have him.

Unfortunately, Khian Walker was my weakness. A weakness that was both a curse and blessing in disguise.

"I want you, Khi," I spoke confidently to him. "I want you just as bad as you want me right now."

That did it for the both of us.

Khian removed his hand from my throat and used both his hands to lift me up. He then locked his soft lips on mine, while carrying me to the sink counter. I was too into us kissing to even care about the sink being damp. His tongue parted my lips and shit got heated between us really fast. His tongue led the way, dominating the passionate and hungry battle of our tongues.

While our tongues battled, so did our hands. His hands were desperate to get my clothes off, ripping my work apron off my body before moving onto my shirt and literally tearing off buttons. The same way he was desperate for my clothes to be off, I was exactly the same way for his. I had already snatched at his Armani belt and pushed his black jeans down his knees, before reaching for the black waistband of his boxers and pulling them down.

I didn't want to waste any time after that. We didn't even have time to waste. As hot as it was, us about to fuck in Club Onyx's restrooms, I didn't want someone to come to the restroom only to complain about it being locked and telling security. Security had the key to unlock the restrooms and I really didn't want to get fired for being alone with Khian instead of being behind the bar, doing my job.

I broke my lips away from Khian, only to help him get my shirt off my shoulders and chunk it to the side. The sound of our heavy breathing filled the room. Our foreheads touched for a moment and my eyes shut as I tried to control the overwhelming lust I could feel growing inside me.

"We need to be quick," I whispered, opening my eyes and wrapping my arms around Khi as he kissed on my neck and pulled my jeans down.

"I know," he replied in between his neck kisses. "But we got... all night... after this."

I frowned, slightly confused with my head tilted to the side so Khian had greater access to my neck. "What do you mean?" I asked, feeling my nerves suddenly build once my thong was down to my ankles.

"I'ma pick you... up after... your shift... and we'll... head back... to yours," he said, continuing to seductively kiss on my skin.

That sure did sound like a plan.

"Okay," I responded meekly.

However, my response had triggered something because instead of wrapping my legs around his torso, Khian stopped kissing on me and lifted his head up from my neck.

"Unless you don't want me to follow you home tonight?"

He was slowly beginning to kill the mood.

"Khian, I never said I didn't want you following me home," I voiced knowingly.

"You sounded li—"

"Are you seriously doing this right now?" I couldn't help but laugh. "You've got me basically naked for you and ready for you to give me your dick."

I was basically naked. My work clothes were to the side and now, I had nothing but my bra on. Khian still had his dark blue t-shirt on and I couldn't help but become turned on with the fact that Khian was still half clothed, yet, I wasn't.

"Do you want me to follow you home though?" he asked curiously.

"Yes," I told him with a sexy smirk, pecking his lips once, before moving down to his neck and kissing him lightly. "I really do."

I felt Khian's hands on my thighs and he wrapped my legs around his torso.

"Ughhh....Khi," I moaned once he had slid into me and began to move rhythmically in and out of me.

"So fuckin' tight," he groaned, gripping tighter around my legs as he thrusted faster, in and out.

"Ahh! Yes!" I whimpered passionately, loving the feeling of his dick moving against my walls. The shit felt so good. Especially since this nigga had the perfect dick. Not too long but certainly not too short either. Thick, wide, and to top it all off - it came with a slight curve. A curve that hit all the right spots whenever he gave it to me.

"Faster," I ordered, digging my nails into his shoulders as my feeling of pleasure grew. "Fuck me fasterrrrrr, yesss!"

He did as I wanted and all I could do was throw my head back in ecstasy as he rammed into me. This was the main reason I couldn't fight away Khian.

Dick too bomb.

CHAPTER 4.

~ Azryah ~

After stripping for the night, I got to the dressing room with my bag of money and opened my locker to get my shit out, including my phone. It was only while reaching for my phone that I heard snickering, but I thought nothing of it until I heard my name.

"Yeah, you know Krystle's wack and highly overrated."

I turned around with my face screwed up into a tight frown.

"Excuse me?"

I was looking at the one bitch in this club that hated to see me win. It's as if seeing me win and make money was the end of the world for her.

"Yeah?"

Ciara aka Peaches, with her dumb, basic ass stage name, stated at me with a conceited smile. She was a pretty girl, I couldn't lie but her personality made her seem ugly. And because she was light skinned, she already felt that she had a different, unique power over everyone.

"You got something you need to say?"

"Nah," she voiced in a sweet voice. "I'm cool."

"Good. Let it stay that way or you might just leave here with a broken fa—"

Before I could finish my threat, Anna entered the room. "Krystle, you're wanted in room nine."

I threw her a strange look.

"Anna, it's the end of my shi—"

"And you already know I don't care," Anna snapped. "Time is money. Get your ass there now."

I sighed deeply, trying to remain as calm as I possibly could. It was 1:30am and all I really wanted right now was my damn bed. But this job wasn't allowing me to have it. Before heading to the room, I checked my phone, knowing I would need to text Michelle and tell her I couldn't drive her back home tonight. To my surprise, she had already texted me.

Don't wait for me. With Khi tonight.

I locked my iPhone, and threw it into my locker along with the bag of money I had placed all my earnings of tonight in. As much as I didn't trust the bitches at this strip club, I knew they would never try to rob my shit. Peaches and all her little minions were scared of my ass, hence why they could never say shit to my face.

Once locking my locker with my padlock, I slipped my key into my tight hair bun before heading to room nine. I was just hoping that whoever had requested for a private dance after my damn shift, was willing to pay extra on the side for holding up my time. I already wasn't looking forward to this dance. Another sleazy ass nigga trying to cop a feel of what would never belong to him. But hey, new day, new money to be made, right? However, upon entering room nine, my feelings about tonight changed completely.

"What are you doing here?"

"Is that anyway to greet your man?"

I scoffed at him in disbelief before folding my arms against my chest as I rested against the door. I didn't like how sexy he was looking, dressed in all black, sitting in a relaxed state on that red, plush leather couch. He wore a black hoodie, black jeans, two silver chains peaking from underneath his hoodie, a silver watch on his wrist that almost blinded my eyes with the amount of diamonds I could see sparkling, and a silver diamond stud in both of his ears. Black was definitely his favorite color because it was the color I saw him in the most. And those tattoos peeking on his neck and on his hands, running up his arms, only appeased me further.

"I wanted to see you, Azryah."

"After you left last time with no reason?"

"I apologize, baby," he sweetly responded. "I just had to figure some shit out."

"And now that you've figured the shit out, you come back here. because?"

"Because I've figured out that I want you and I don't want anyone else to have you but me."

Damn, I wasn't expecting him to say all that. But now he had said it, a wave of joy had flown through my body.

"But how do you know that I even want you?"

"'Cause I know how wet I make you, I know how much I turn you on, and I know that you can't stop thinking about me. The same way I can't stop thinking about you."

"You hardly know me," I told him with a roll of my eyes. "You can't possibly know all that."

"Well, I wanna get to know you and I ain't takin' no for an answer this time."

From the look in his eyes, I could tell that he was dead ass serious about wanting to get to know me. And could I really reject him again for the second time? I didn't see the crime in letting him try to get to know me. I had been trying to get his attention from the second I had seen him, so what else did I think it was gonna lead to?

"Okay... one date."

The smile on his face was bright enough to light up the whole room.

***

Last night, we both agreed on him taking me to Cheesecake Factory. I didn't want to go to any place fancy, I just wanted to eat. So Cheesecake Factory was the perfect place. Right now, it was 11:30am and I had just woken up. Kaylen was coming to get me at 5pm and I was cool with that. I had decided already that I most definitely wasn't going into work today. I just wanted today to be a really nice chill day, including the date with Kaylen later on. "Nice, chill day" quickly took a turn for the worse when I stepped into the kitchen to see two horny lovers tonguing each other down.

"Yo, please get a room," I voiced in a time filled with disgust, as I walked past them to head to the fridge.

I had woken up with a strong desire for apple juice and toast this morning, so that's what I was going to have. Once I had opened the fridge, the cool breeze hit me and I got out my apple juice before shutting the fridge.

"Good morning to you too, gurl," Michelle greeted me in an amused tone.

I turned around to see her standing by the kitchen sink, grinning at me, while Khian had his arms wrapped around her waist as he lightly kissed her neck. Jealousy decided to hit at me again, but I shot it away as I thought about my date with Kaylen later on.

"What's good about it?" I negatively queried, turning back round to walk towards the brown cupboards that contained the glasses.

"Absolutely everything," Michelle said in a tone that sounded like she had been given way too much dick over the past twenty-four hours. I wouldn't be surprised if she ended up pregnant soon, with the way they went at it.

"I'm gonna hop in the shower, Khi," Michelle informed him in a happy tone. "You're welcome to join me." She giggled lightly like some damn teenager with some high school crush.

"I might just have to take you up on that offer," he sexually responded.

Michelle giggled, then departed the kitchen and I decided to keep my back turned while taking a sip of the apple juice I had poured.

"Yo, Azryah."

I slowly turned around to face him. Staring at him with curiosity as I lifted my cup off my lips.

"Yeah?"

"So, I'm guessin' you like my twin," he said simply. "Word of advice, don't play around with him. He's not like any type of average guy you've been with in the past."

"Who on earth said anything about me liking him?"

He smirked before asking, "So you don't like him then?"

I shyly looked down, not wanting him to see the truth in my eyes. Of course I liked Kaylen. I couldn't help it. No seriously, I really couldn't. This just wasn't about how he looked but it was the way he carried himself, almost as if he was royalty.

"That's what I thought," Khian knowingly stated. "Look, for what it's worth, I know he really likes you too. As far as he's concerned in his head, you're already his girl."

"No, I'm not," I disagreed, staring back up at him. I privately thought about how good he looked shirtless and prayed that Kaylen looked the same. Or better yet, ten times sexier shirtless than Khian did.

"Yes, you are his girl now, even if he hasn't claimed you verbally yet and you haven't gotten to know him that well, vice versa. You're still his girl, Azryah, just take my advice and don't play around with his emotions. I know my twin like the back of my hand."

"That's cool and all, but I'm not his girl."

"Azryah, you most definitely are."

Even when I tried to explain that I wasn't Kaylen's girl, he wasn't allowing me. He was crazy though. I wasn't Kaylen's girl.

~ *Azryah* ~

"Why do you keep staring at me?"

"Why do you think?" he questioned me curiously. "You dress like this to our date and you think a nigga not gon' stare at your fine ass?"

With a simple sentence, he already had me blushing. I really didn't like how quickly he could have my emotions running high for him. I didn't like it one bit. As agreed, he had taken me to the Cheesecake Factory, picked me up in his Maserati at eight o'clock sharp, and driven us both here. Him, sitting opposite me and staring at me as if I was something on the damn menu, had me nervous, I couldn't lie. I knew wearing this short dress was gonna have me in trouble tonight because the look in Kaylen's eyes told me one thing and one thing only...

He wanted me.

"What made you start stripping?" he asked me out of the blue, in the middle of us eating.

"I needed some more cash," I simply explained. "Was the easiest way for me to get some."

"So you didn't have any other goals or dreams before stripping?"

"No."

"Seriously?" he asked in a surprised tone. "None?"

I shook my head no and carried on eating, praying that he would stop with all the talking for a bit. He didn't. I didn't want to talk about my past, it tended to make me feel emotional.

"Tryna get money's cool and all, but it's not cool when you haven't got any goals or aspirations to go alongside it, Azryah. No woman of mine is gonna live a goalless life. I get that you love stripping but you gotta do something more meaningful with your life, something respectful and valuable to yourself as a woman. 'Cause stripping ain't gonna cut it anymore."

By the sounds of things, it sounded like Kaylen was telling me that I had to quit stripping and do something else.

"Wait... what are you saying?"

"I'm saying..." He paused talking momentarily so he could grab his napkin and pat his mouth clean from any food particles. "You need to quit stripping."

I dropped my fork with rage and cut my eyes at him. I was pissed because Kaylen thought that because of this one date, he was automatically the boss of me. When he really and truly wasn't.

"Cut your eyes all you want, baby, but don't get mad 'cause you know I'm speaking sense."

"You aren't speakin' sense," I retorted. "I'm not quitting my job, my source of income. How am I supposed to eat?"

"Now look at the one who ain't speakin' sense," he commented smugly, gazing deeply at me. "I always take care of mines, you ain't gotta worry about anything."

"Uh-uh," I disagreed with a stern head shake. "I ain't yours and even if I was, I ain't never gon' need a man to take care of me."

"There it is," he declared with a chuckle.

"What?" I threw him a frown.

"I see what listening to too much Beyoncé and Nicki Minaj has done to you."

I was confused by his point.

"Girls don't run the world," he explained with a silly smirk. "You're just gassed up into thinkin' that shit but it ain't true."

"Well, a man certainly doesn't run my world," I fumed. "Never have and never will."

"So, you won't let me run your heart?"

Even though I was pissed at his mind filled with patriarchy, I was slightly smitten by his last question. It was corny but still cute and romantic.

"Kaylen..." I threw him a weary look. I didn't know if I could really allow him to get his hopes up, thinking that one day I would be the mother of his children because trust me, I wasn't.

"A nigga tryna show you that he cares and you keep pushing him away," he announced in an irritated tone. "Can't you see that I'm trying to get to know you on a much deeper level? Can't you see that I'm tryna make you mine?"

"You're just tryna get in my pants," I muttered casually.

"And, so what if I am?" he cockily questioned me. "Damn right, I'm tryna get in those panties but I'm not rushing shit, because I want to get to know you properly. I want to get to know every single little detail before I slide up inside you. I don't want you thinkin' that a nigga just gon' hit it and quit it 'cause I ain't. Trust me."

The look in his eyes as he stared deeply at me, told me one thing only - he was being completely serious.

"Azryah, look," he began in a softer tone as he flicked his tongue across his lips. A flick that made my heart skip a beat. "I'm tryna get to know you, every single part of your pretty ass. That includes your personality, your body, your interests, your dislikes... everything, baby. You just need to open up and let me in. Ain't no need to hide, I'm not gonna hurt you."

"And what if you do?" I asked him in a curious tone. "If you hurt me, then that means you're nothing but a liar."

"I'm not gonna hurt you," he explained, moving his hand across the table closer towards me. "I promise."

I looked down at his open palm that was reaching out for me and then back up at him, into those brown mesmerizing eyes, then down that body as I admired how he was dressed tonight, a simple beige blazer with a white shirt inside, black jeans, and black Balenciaga's to match. He was too fine for his own good and way too fine for me not to stare at him.

Eventually, I decided to stop fighting him and give in. So I placed my hand in his and let him hold it up before placing it to his lips. All the while, he kept his eyes on me.

A clever charmer indeed.

***

"I had a great time tonight with you, girl."

"Can't lie and say that I didn't enjoy myself too... A little bit."

"You got jokes, you know that, right?"

"Hmm... I've been told."

"So, when you gon' let your nigga take you out again?"

"Whenever he likes?"

And that's how it happened.

Khian's words of me being Kaylen's girl happened quicker than I had expected. Shit happened so fast, I didn't even notice. Kaylen was just taking me everywhere he could and it got to the point that there wasn't a single day where we didn't see each other. It also got to the point that I couldn't go into my night shifts at Club Onyx anymore. Because

a) I was too tired from my date with Kaylen from the previous night or b) He was taking me some place new the same night.

"Anna's been asking about you. Should I tell her you're not coming back?" Michelle questioned me suspiciously as she looked at me put my earrings on.

It had been two weeks exactly since I had last worked at Club Onyx. I was more surprised that Anna hadn't told Michelle that my ass was fired, but instead, she was asking about me as if I was on a little holiday or illness bedrest.

"I need to go see her," I responded coolly as I reached for my mascara wand to curl my natural lashes slightly more.

"To tell her you still want your job?"

Despite me saying that I would never need a man to take care of me, Kaylen was doing exactly that and taking care of me. Before I could even object, he would stuff a few bands into my purse at the end of our dates, after pulling up to my apartment complex. He wasn't the easiest person to refuse either. So me trying to give him back his money was a no-go zone.

"No," I stated. "To tell her I'm done."

"You're done?" Michelle threw me a strange look while questioning me. "You're done with stripping?"

I couldn't believe the words that were actually about to leave my mouth. But this was now the reality of my life. "I'm done with stripping."

"What?" she shockingly asked, continuing to examine me carefully. "Are you sure?"

I nodded simply before looking back into the mirror in front of me and examining my appearance.

"Wow, I guess I'll let her know," Michelle voiced coolly before deciding to depart my bedroom.

I didn't realize how grateful I was that she had decided to give me some personal space, until my phone lit up on my dresser in front of me, alerting me of the new text notification. One glance at my phone and a small grin grew on my lips.

I'm seein' you tonight shorty. Wear that sexy shit like you always do.

I picked up my phone and entered in my passcode before heading straight to my messages, typing up my response before quickly sending it.

Tonight? I've gotta check my diary and see if I'm free.

Within an instant, he responded: *Oh, it's like that huh?*

I bit my lips as I pictured him licking his lips while thinking about me. Damn, this nigga had me smitten without even being next to me.

Me: What can I say? I'm a busy woman.

Kaylen: Quit playin' girl. You ain't never too busy for your man.

Kaylen: Besides you know how busy a nigga gonna get in the next coming days. Just get ready and I'ma come pick you up.

Me: Kaylen, I don't know... I really do have plans for tonight.

I didn't but shit, he really didn't need to know that.

Kaylen: Cancel them.

Kaylen: I'm seeing you tonight.

Me: You've seen me every single other night. Why aren't you bored of me yet?

Instead of getting a fast response from him right away, I received nothing. And it wasn't until my phone screen locked out that it suddenly brightened up again and vibrated due to the FaceTime request, from Mr. Kaylen Walker.

Butterflies filled my stomach as my finger moved towards the green answer button, and before I knew it, Kaylen's handsome face appeared on my screen.

"Is your ass retarded or something?"

I immediately scrunched my face up at his rude question, not to mention his arrogant tone.

"Excuse me?" I asked him in a tone filled with disapproval.

"You heard me," he stated boldly with a smirk, while finessing his fingers through his light chin beard. "Quit playin', Az. I'm dead ass serious about seeing you tonight."

From what I could see on my screen, Kaylen was chilling on his couch, completely shirtless and unbothered about the fact that I was seeing his tatted-up chest. The heating building between my thighs was going to turn into a problem very soon. I just knew it.

"Kaylen...I—"

"Uh-uh, shut up," he retorted, making me frown with disgust. "You got one hour, baby girl."

"After you just told me to shut up, you think I'm still following you anywhere?"

His smirk grew and he licked his lips in that sexy way that always made me breathless.

Fuck.

"One hour," he instructed bossily before winking at me seductively and ending the FaceTime call.

He was trouble and I knew it, but that only made me want to pursue him more.

CHAPTER 5

~ *Kaylen* ~

*M*iss me?

Maybe, she responded.

Me: Nah you definitely do. I'ma slide through later on tonight. Around like 8?

Azryah: Alrightie, sounds good.

Like, what the hell was she doing to me?

It didn't matter what day it was, what time of the day it was, and where I was, if I wanted to see her then I was seeing her. To make matters worse, because I wasn't pressing her for sex, I couldn't stop having dreams about her sexy ass. And every single one only blew my mind further and kept growing my lustful plans list for her. We weren't even in a serious relationship but it sure felt that's where we were heading. Even more so that I had started spending the night at her crib whenever I came back from a long day working, hustling and shit, as per usual.

Azryah was yet to know about my profession. All she knew

was that a nigga was rich and could take her of her pretty ass. That's all I wanted her to know from the start because I knew how sketchy and dodgy things could get if I started mixing my business life with personal. And could I even trust her well enough to know about the fact that I was moving weight, owning large territories, and constantly fighting off my enemies and let's not forget the cops.

The mighty, brave cops, constantly on my back and radar, wanting to know what I was up to and how I was becoming so rich. They had already stressed me last year, trying to turn one of my boys against me and offering to pay him millions if he snitched on me. Of course, Jacob wasn't no snitch, but even when he was eventually left alone, I had to get rid of him because I knew that he was toying with the possibility of selling me out. And say we got into an argument one day, who's to say that I could trust him not to go running to the cops out of anger?

Telling Azryah about my business as a drug dealer wasn't something that I could see myself doing. Maybe in a couple years' time, after getting myself out of this crazy lifestyle, I would let her know but for now, hell no. I figured she probably did have an idea of what I did but didn't know the full extent. And she didn't ask questions whenever I was stuffing racks of cash in her purse. Shit, I didn't blame her. Money was money, regardless of where it came from.

Her not asking questions however, kept me a calm, tranquil state of mind, not worrying about having to dig myself into a big lie to cover up my tracks. I was fine. I just prayed that she didn't get curious anytime soon because I really wasn't prepared to start lying to her.

I really did like Azryah. Azryah Jones. Shit, I even liked her name but the sound of her being Azryah Walker, I loved more.

And there it was. Me talking crazy again. I may have been claiming her as my girl already but we weren't in a serious relationship yet. But already here I was thinking about giving her my last name. How sway?

I didn't even feel like I knew her well enough. Sure, I had asked her plenty of questions about her childhood, her family, her hobbies, and interests, but still I felt like I didn't know the real her.

There was a deeper, hidden layer to Azryah that I was close to uncovering. I just had to keep on playing my role and being a gentleman to her. It wasn't even about me trying to get into her panties because believe me, if that's all I wanted after all these weeks, I would have gotten it already. It was about me getting to know this girl that I was so interested in. Getting to know a side of her that no one else knew of. Getting to know beyond that stripper persona she had created.

Only God knew how pleased I was that I had managed to get her to stop stripping. Now that I was becoming more serious about pursuing her, there's no way I would have felt comfortable with her stripping for some sleazy ass niggas. I really didn't need anyone looking at my girl and lusting over her half naked body. That was for me to do only.

Knock! Knock!

After a long day of grinding, the only person on my mind was her. She was the only face I wanted to see, the only voice I wanted to hear. I would say the only lips I wanted to kiss but the funny thing about our little situation was that we hadn't kissed since that night she gave me a private lap dance at Club Onyx. She had only given a nigga a few cheek kisses and I had given her forehead kisses. But full-blown tongue action, yeah, we were no way near that stage again. It felt foreign to me too. Making me feel like some inexperienced teenage boy, knowing fully well that I was beyond experienced. I had made the prettiest chicks become wet with one wink of my eye.

"Kaylen," Michelle greeted me warmly as she opened the door wide for me. Her eyes looking me up and down with a grin. "What a pleasant surprise."

I hadn't seen Azryah for approximately three days and two nights. Only because like I said, a nigga been busy grinding and hustling. I also didn't want any distractions while working and Azryah Jones was a major distraction. Because if it were up to me, I'd be texting and Face Timing her ass all day long instead of getting any work done.

"What's up, Michelle?" I gave her a simple smile while stepping deeper into their apartment.

Azryah's roommate seemed like cool peoples. Azryah didn't have no problems with her, so I guessed I had no problems with her either.

"Nothing much, you ain't been around in a minute," Michelle commented with curious eyes.

I nodded at her before responding, "Yeah, I've been busy, I can't lie. But I came through finally to see my baby girl."

Michelle's grin grew wider as she continued to stare at me. Shorty was bad, I couldn't lie. But her attractiveness did nothing to me because of how hooked I was onto Azryah. Also, Khian was fucking around with Michelle. So she was completely off limits.

"Well, it's good to see you," she concluded before walking past me in the direction of the kitchen. "She's in her room napping, by the way."

"A'ight, thanks," I stated casually before heading in the opposite direction, towards the carpeted stairs leading to her bedroom upstairs.

Once finally making it up the stairs, I walked to her bedroom door and quietly pushed it open.

The first thing I laid eyes on was the beautiful goddess lying peacefully in her bed, indeed sleeping. She wasn't a heavy snorer either, so there were no noises coming from her.

I decided to slip my sneakers off by her door and move closer to her bed. I pulled back her covers, and gently crept onto the empty bedside, and positioned myself right next to her. Wrapping my arm around her bare waist only to realize now that she was wearing a crop top and booty shorts. The kind of booty shorts that made her ass look perfect and those thighs even sexier.

Damn, it felt so good being next to her right now.

I definitely got lost with touching her because I shifted closer to her on the bed and that resulted in her waking up. Her eyes popped open in fear and she suddenly turned around to see the intruder who was holding onto her. But turning around to see my eyes looking down at her made her hard, cold facial expression instantly soften.

"Kaylen... God, you scared me," she voiced quietly, sighing softly. She turned her face away from me. I lightly chuckled at her previous fearful state, before resting my neck on her shoulder and kissing the nook of her neck.

"Sorry, sweetheart," I apologized in a low whisper. "Your ass almost scared me with that loud ass snoring though."

She let out a loud giggle before lightly nudging me with her elbow. "Kay, you know damn well I don't snore."

I grinned before saying, "Yeah, I know, but a nigga still gotta tease you from time to time."

She scoffed before shutting her eyes and snuggling her body closer to mine. "I low-key missed you," she admitted.

"I know," I cockily replied before adding, "I low-key missed you too."

"I mean, who else am I gonna get to take me out and buy me dinner? All my side niggas are unavailable right now."

"Wow," I said with a chuckle. "So you've been using me all this time for some food?"

"Yup," she amusingly responded. "A girl's gotta eat!"

"You scammer," I joked. "I've seen your true colors indeed."

She loudly giggled before asking, "Were you planning to take me out tonight?"

"Nope! But I'm sure your side niggas can take you out, right?" I tightened my hold around her waist and lifted my lips up from her neck. "Besides, I kinda just wanted to chill with you at home tonight."

"Hmm," she hummed before turning her body around in her position, to face me completely. My arm left her waist and I waited until she had shifted herself before placing a grip back on her. "Sounds good."

Staring down into her pretty brown eyes only made me want to kiss her. Over three weeks of seeing each other and we were still yet to kiss again. The shit really didn't make sense to me. But just as I made a move to press my lips down to hers, Azryah dropped a bombshell.

"I went back to Club Onyx two days ago," she revealed.

I gave her a strange look. "Why the fuck did you do that?"

"To hand in my ID card and locker key."

I instantly sighed a sigh of relief. She began to lightly laugh at me.

"Yo, that shit wasn't funny," I playfully snapped. "I really was about to fuck you up for disobeying me."

Her eyes widened with surprise. "Fuck me up? Yeah, in your dreams. You know I know karate."

"And none of that goofy ninja shit woulda saved your ass," I told her with a cheeky grin. "But for real though, you really went to drop your ID card and shit?" I needed to know that she definitely hadn't started back stripping.

She nodded reassuringly, while looking up at me confidently. That was all the confirmation I needed about the situation. As long as she wasn't stripping again, we were completely Gucci.

"A'ight, cool," I responded coolly. "So from now on, anytime you feel like stripping, you just strip for me."

"What?" She laughed heartily. "Umm, Kaylen, no."

"Why not?" I shot a raised brow at her with a suspicious look. "None of your side niggas get the privilege of seeing your fine ass half naked or getting private lap dances anymore. That's all mine now."

"But me quitting stripping means quitting it completely."

"Yeah, you're quitting it for money making purposes but not for pleasing your man," I reminded her. "Shit, if you want a nigga to make it rain on you a couple times while you dance for me, then I have no problems doing that. Anything to make you happy and besides, that shit will look sexy as fuck."

I looked on as she began to blush, shyly looking down away from my eyes. Even after all the time we had been spending together, she would still become coy around me. The whole act she had been putting on with me when we first met had been a layer to her that I had managed to unlock. Beneath all that attitude, was a shy woman who needed the right man to experience her inner freak. That man was most definitely me.

"Kaylen... In regards to money," she spoke up in a low, unconfident tone all of a sudden. She was still avoiding eye contact with me and it was making me slightly irritated. "I'm gonna look for a jo—"

"No the fuck you ain't," I cut across her speech, grabbing her chin, and forcing her to look up at me. "You don't need to ever worry about working because I told you, I got you."

She pushed my hand off her chin. "But, Kaylen, I don't want to dep—"

"What the fuck did I just say?" I fumed, cutting my eyes at her. "I got you. You don't need to worry about anything else."

"I don't know how you think looking after my finances when we're not in a serious relationship is a good thing," she quickly blurted out and seeing that I wasn't interrupting her this time, she continued. "We're getting to know each other, yes, but that's just it, we're still getting to know each other. I have no real idea about your job and how you're getting all this money. I know you're involved with drugs, Kaylen... but how? Why?"

And there it was.

The questions I had been dreading from her. The questions that I knew were going to change everything. Either I let her know the truth, or I cut her off and forget this whole situation occurred. But even I couldn't bring myself to think about the second option. Leaving Azryah was not an option. I wasn't surprised about her knowing about me being a drug dealer because eventually she was gonna put two and two together like everybody else did.

"Az... I don't want you worrying about shit that don't concern you," I explained coldly, slightly loosening my hold on her waist. "Some things are just better left unsaid."

She pouted at me before replying, "You can't keep calling yourself my man if you won't let me find out about the real you. The real Kaylen."

"But you are seeing the real Kaylen," I insisted. "A Kaylen that no other bitches get to see. You think I take all these girls on dates the way I'm taking you? You think I'm paying their bills? You think I'm laying up in their bed having deep convos and shit? You think I wait this long to fuck?"

"I'm not seeing the real Kaylen if you can't come clean and honest to me about your profession," she retorted. "You're hiding shit from me and claim this is the real you. Like, don't you fucking get it?"

"Watch that damn mouth, yo," I warned her with a tense look "You just don't need to know about what I do right now, Az. It's way too early. Just give a nigga time and I promise, I'll come around. But for the meantime, just continue to let me look after you and treat yo—"

"No, that isn't gonna work, Kaylen."

"Huh?"

"It isn't gonna work," she repeated rudely. "You don't trust me enough to tell me the truth. Then you really need to get the hell out and leave me al—"

"And what'd I just tell you about that damn mouth?"

She sucked her teeth quietly before attempting to roll over to the other side, away from me. But I instantly grabbed a grip on her waist again, which forced her to stay put in front of me. Seeing her give me a dirty look, only made my frustrations with her build.

"What'd I tell you about that mouth, girl?"

"I really don't give a fuc—"

But before she could continue throwing insults towards me, I captured her lips into a deep, hungry kiss. A kiss that had been long overdue. Even she knew it too because she didn't bother trying to push me off her, she submissively kissed me back.

Shit started getting heated pretty fast after seeing that she was down with letting a nigga kiss her. It was as if fireworks had been let off and bright lights were sparkling all around us. My heart filled with an indescribable feeling as I pulled her closer towards me and parted her lips with my tongue. Beginning to erotically dance my tongue with hers, slowly and sensually allowing her to savor every second of the kiss. My tongue dominated her mouth, colliding and battling with hers, letting her know that I wasn't one to be played with. And when a soft moan escaped her lips between the kiss, I knew for sure that she was officially hooked. She was officially hooked onto me.

While our tongues meshed, my hands gently massaged her soft skin and it wasn't long 'til my hands ran across her back before sliding down to her firm, round ass. *Smack!*

"Mmh!" Again, her moan escaped past the seal of our lips, and I gently rubbed away the slight sting I had caused on her butt. We were still intimately kissing, neither one of us looking to stop soon. One thing she was now going to be able to add to her list about me was that I was great at multitasking.

"Hmm... mmh... Ka...Kay," her gentle moans continued to sound and I could feel my dick getting hard. It was time to stop before things went to the next level. Before I ended up fucking her tied to the bedposts with nowhere to run or hide from me.

When I pulled our lips apart, I heard her groan and even I realized that ending our kiss so soon was a mistake. But I quickly redeemed myself, settling my face on the side of her neck and carefully planting pecks on her skin. Even beginning to form love bites, officially marking my territory.

"Whoa, Kay," she groaned in a tone mixed with pleasure and pain. She was going to quickly catch on that those were two feelings I always brought into the bedroom. "Fuuck."

"What... I tell you... about that mouth?" I queried in a pleased tone in between my kisses on the bites I had just left. Mostly pleased that she was enjoying the pleasure and pain I provided.

"I... I...."

I decided to seductively lick her skin and then deciding that the party was over for now. It was time to get back to normal. I came up from Azryah's neck and stared at the lustful expression written all over her gorgeous face.

"Oh, so you quiet now, huh? Nah, don't play yourself now, speak up. You had so much to say before, right?" I cockily asked. "Well let me say this, you'll find out all about me, Az, I promise you that. But you just gotta be patient with a nigga 'cause this is all brand new to me. I don't date girls, I just fuck 'em. But I don't just wanna fuck you 'cause I'm really digging you, baby girl."

She shot me a gleaming smile before nodding contently.

"I have one request though."

"And what's that?"

"I don't want you to stop kissing me right now."

I carefully listened to her request and observed as she sexually bit her lips at me. We weren't about to have sex but she knew exactly what was going down. If she wasn't hooked before, she was most definitely hooked now.

***

Me: I'm in trouble bro.

Khian: What why?

Me: I'm falling in love with her. What if it kills me?

Khian: Kay if you don't get your dumb ass to sleep.

Me: I'm dead ass serious bro, I texted him as I looked behind me to see Azryah sleeping peacefully.

Khian: You won't die, shut up. See this as good thing. At least now you can stop going around and actin' like a little hoe. Embrace it. That's the girl you gon' marry 'cause ain't no female you talked to me about in this way.

Me: I know and that's the shit that scares me the most. I haven't felt like this in a very long time. She's special man.

Khian: Just keep things the way they are and see where they go. And don't fuck it up.

Me: Yeah bro.

Me: I'ma get some sleep, so night nigga.

Khian: Wait... where are you?

Me: I'm at her crib.

Khian: Well damn... you sprung for real.

Me: Yeah I guess I am. She fell asleep in my arms too and that shit had me feeling butterflies.

Khian: Ha! Nigga this is only the start.

Me: I know. Shit's only gonna get even more real between us. And guess what?

Khian: What?

Me: Still ain't fucked her.

Khian: Dead ass?

Me: Dead ass.

Khian: Wow... you really are in love, aren't you?

Me: Yeah man... I really am.

~ *Khian* ~

Today, Kaylen and I were gonna spend the day with some of our homies. Just chilling and having fun, like we usually did every month. Our cousin, CJ, was having a kickback today and I was actually looking forward to that shit. Because it meant that we could be away from females and just hang out with my cousin and our close homies.

Don't get me wrong, I had no problems with the female in my life. Matter fact, shit between Michelle and me was just fine. We were fucking around from time to time when I wasn't busy and when I could come over to her crib. She understood our situation and didn't try forcing shit between us. She had definitely stopped all the clingy texts she used to send whenever I went ghost on her. Now she just knew what it was and accepted it.

Even though today was just supposed to be a regular ass Saturday with just the boys, I hadn't seen Michelle in over a week now. I was missing her low-key and I most definitely missed that pussy. So, I decided to holla at her and see if she was free for me to come see her real quick.

I shot her a quick text, praying that she would reply quickly. I was already dressed for the kick back in my black Timberlands, denim jeans, and fresh white tee. I was a simple guy, I couldn't lie. Simple or not, I always looked good.

Michelle: *I'm heading out soon Khi.*

I rolled my eyes at her message before responding, *I won't take up much of your time, sweetheart. I just wanna see you.*

Michelle: *Why?*

Khian: *You know why. I miss my girls.*

Michelle: *Your girls?*

Khian: *You and my pussy.*

Khian: *Just let me slide through real quick. Promise you I'll make it worth your while.*

Michelle: *Okay...*

Michelle: *Hurry up.*

***

"Agh... Got damn it, Mich... you fuckin' killing me," I groaned, watching as Michelle continued to ride and bounce on my dick. I was just moments from cumming and she knew that shit too, which is why she was constantly changing up her speeds. She had already got hers, so she was just toying with a nigga now. One minute, she would go super-fast but then she could tell that I was close to busting, so then she would slow shit down completely. "Fuuuuuck."

"You ready to cum or what?" she teasingly asked, seductively biting her lips before lifting her hands off my chest and playing with her large tits through her see-through crop top. And she definitely knew how turned on I always got seeing her play with herself in front of me.

Then she increased her momentum once more, quickly lifting herself up and down my hard shaft. From the speed, to seeing her breasts bounce up and down and the looks of pleasure sweeping across her face, I was more than ready to cum.

"Shit, ugh," I whimpered, finally releasing my load into the Trojan wrapped around my dick. Even as I was climaxing, this freak didn't stop riding me. It was like she was trying to take my soul out of me and claim it as her own.

Next shit she did, almost made a nigga start crying. I wasn't no cry baby though; my eyes just became watery but the tears stayed put in my lids.

"Got damn it, Mich... you are... one nasty ass bitch," I commented in a lustful tone, observing as she had slipped her pussy off my dick, removed the Trojan, and had now put her mouth on my wet tip.

My dick was completely drenched in my cum, edging her on further. The second her lips made contact with my length, she sucked me dry. Keeping both eyes on me, completely as she ate up my dick, knowing fully well that her doing shit like this drove a nigga wild. She was using no hands too and it was truly a skill of hers I admired greatly.

"Mich... oh, shit." Her head was bobbing vigorously up and down nonstop as her lips popped on and off me. Hearing her begin to choke as she sucked faster only took me closer and closer to another euphoric high.

The tears that had been sitting so comfortably in my lids decided to escape when Michelle popped her lips off my manhood and slowly trickled her saliva on the tip. Watching her let it fall on my tip and run against my veiny shaft was a sight that I never saw as sexy until now. She raised one hand to rub and massage her spit all along my dick before sloppily slurping it all up like it was nothing. Like she hadn't just gone all extra freaky on me.

A few minutes later, we were both spent. And while Michelle slept on her front with no covers hiding her lower body from me, I got dressed. My eyes stayed sealed to her butt though and the way it was still looking so juicy, even though I had already tapped that.

"I'ma hit you up later," I announced just as I pulled my shirt over my head.

"Uh-huh," she softly responded, sounding tired as hell.

"Thanks for making a nigga feel good."

"Uh-huh," she repeated, followed by a quiet exhale. "No problem, Khi."

Once I was completely dressed, I went closer to her bedside, pecked her cheek, and left. I had wasted quite some with Michelle already, to the fact that I was officially late for the kickback. My phone had been on do not disturb but when I turned it on, the flood of missed calls and texts messages that had come in were no joke.

Mostly, CJ had blown up my phone with various text messages and calls. My only goal right now was to get to the kickback and have a good time. I simply shot him a text that I was on my way and headed to his. Praying that these niggas hadn't raided all the food already.

Forty minutes later and I had arrived at the kickback. To my surprise, Kaylen's Lambo was already in CJ's driveway and loud upbeat rap music filled my eardrums. I hadn't expected him to get there before me because this nigga loved to make an entrance all the time.

So, imagine my surprise, when I walked into CJ's backyard to see

Kaylen sitting on a garden bench with Azryah on his lap.

Yeah, you read correctly.

Azryah was on his lap. Holding him and giggling, while he whispered into her ear. I couldn't help but grin as I stared at Kaylen's happiness. My brother was officially a taken man.

"Yo, who told your bro to mess up the no chicks allowed rule?" Curtis asked me as he walked up to me, Corona in hand and passed it to me.

I willingly accepted it while still looking at Azryah and Kaylen, who were far too engrossed in each other to focus on me and the guys looking at them.

"Man, I don't know," I stated coolly before taking a swig of my drink. "I can't wait to hear this big ass speech he's gonna do though."

"How you know he's gonna make a speech?" CJ inquired.

"'Cause he's my twin. I know him more than I know myself."

A few minutes later, my words were proven right. Kaylen gave me a head nod and a goofy smirk before pulling Azryah in front of him and wrapping his arms around her waist.

"Yo, everyone! I got someone I needa introduce to you all," he announced calmly, pressing a peck to Azryah's cheek after speaking.

While his eyes darted around, staring into the curious eyes of our cousin and the guys. "Guys, this is Azryah," Kaylen stated in an outgoing voice, slightly tightening his grip around her. "My girl."

A few of the guys nodded while others couldn't believe it. Lakeith, for example, didn't believe it and wasn't afraid to voice his feelings.

"Your girl? Nigga, are you sure you ain't fallen and bumped your head somewhere? We all know you ain't no one woman man," he jokingly commented, resulting in everyone to chuckle including me.

Kaylen couldn't help but crack a smile and neither could Azryah, by the looks of it. But then, he spoke up even more and changed everyone's opinions about the situation.

"Yeah, but that was the old Kay. The new Kay has finally found someone, he believes he could potentially spend the rest of his life with. And I know what you're all thinkin', you're all like family to Khian and I, so I expect the worry and the apprehension but look, Azryah and I are cool. We've been kicking it for more than a month now and just really been enjoying each other. And I know all of you are shocked 'cause she used to strip and now I'm with her, but all that shit is in the past and don't fuckin' matter to me, all I want to do is be with her. She wants a nigga too, so this isn't some one-sided shit."

"Well damn, is Azryah gon' ever get to speak up? Baby girl, you good there? Blink twice if you need us to come save you from this fool," Lakeith joked again and everyone happily laughed, while I remained frozen.

Kaylen had just spoken in a way that I had never heard from my twin before. Like Lakeith just said, Kay was not a one-woman man. If he wanted a chick, then he was having her and even after having her, a new chick came along. Then he was having her too. That's just the way he always had been and I really never expected that Kaylen to change. Until now that Azryah had come into his life. He was definitely right about him falling in love. At first, I thought he might have been joking but he really wasn't.

This nigga was in love.

"Yeah, I speak," she shyly spoke up, those pretty brown eyes examining each man looking right back at her. "Hi. I'm Kaylen's girlfriend, like he just said. And yes, I know Kaylen was a bit of a hoe before me."

The guys heartily laughed at her comment, CJ yelling out, "A bit more than a hoe!" Resulting in Kaylen playfully cutting his eyes at him, before staring back down at Azryah in his arms.

"But like he said, that's all in the past and I'm really just ready to focus on the future. Kaylen wanted me to meet you guys because he said you're all his family, even though you're not bound together by blood, he feels connected to you guys."

CJ, Lakeith, Devonte, Curtis, Ray, and Bryant - Kaylen and I's mutual homies since high school and 'til this day, we were still all so close. So bringing Azryah around them was something serious. Extremely serious because it meant that Kaylen trusted her and expected us all to trust her too.

"So I'm really hoping you guys will be willing to accept me in and trust in what Kaylen and I are growing together," she concluded before turning up to look at Kaylen. He instantly pecked her lips before whispering something to her.

Things were silent for a while before the guys started drawing in closer to her and Kaylen. I willingly followed them, moving closer to the happy couple.

"Course we gon' accept you in girl," CJ assured her. "You family now."

All I could do was widely smile at Kaylen when he made eye contact with me and speak up once CJ was done talking.

"CJ's right," I agreed confidently. "You family now."

Azryah made Kay happy. She was something special because no other girl had a hold on him. He usually just fucked chicks and left them alone. However, he and Azryah hadn't even smashed yet from what he had told me. There wasn't a doubt in my mind telling me that Azryah wasn't the perfect girl for my brother. Because she was and I knew that shit 100%.

CHAPTER 6

~ *Azryah* ~

Don't get me wrong, I knew who Kaylen Walker was. I had heard multiple stories about him and I knew he was a dangerous guy. I knew he killed those who crossed him and I knew he didn't play about his money. The funny thing was, I had yet to see one ounce of the Kaylen I had heard so much about. All I was seeing and experiencing was a softer side to him. A side I could tell that not everyone got to see.

And it's like he didn't want me to see the real Kaylen. The murderer Kaylen. The ruthless Kaylen. The thug Kaylen. He just wanted me to see soft Kaylen nonstop and even when he got mad around me, the shit wasn't for long.

I had heard some of his quick phone calls. Him warning those who worked for him not to piss him off and get what he wanted done, ASAP. But that was really about it. Was I really trying to see that darker side of his? I didn't think I would be able to handle it.

"We're here, baby girl," Kaylen sweetly announced while pulling up into the driveway of a fairly medium sized house. A house that I knew just couldn't be his only one. With the wealth I knew he had, there was no way that this was his only house. But this was him opening up to me, so I was going to accept it as his only spot, for now.

Like I said, it was a medium sized house with a large front garden space. Inside, I was greeted to an all-white interior with beige furniture to match. The flooring in his front foyer and lounge was a rich, dark mahogany. Only difference in the lounge was the fact that he had a Persian rug centered in the room. A rug that looked like it cost a fortune because of its large size and exquisite patterns. Mounted on the wall in front of his white loveseat recliner was a 50-inch TV screen and underneath a nicely set up stand with speakers, his game console, and controllers.

It was simple but I could definitely tell it was all Kaylen. All Kaylen's style. Although I was still fully aware of him having more than one home.

"You okay?" he queried curiously, as he took a seat next to me on the loveseat. "You seem a little... off?"

I shook my head no as a response before saying, "I'm cool."

"No you're not," he stated firmly, sliding a hand onto my thigh. "What's wrong?"

"I mean..." my words trailed off as I tried to break eye contact with him, not wanting to stare into those appealing eyes any longer. "I'm fine, Kay—"

My chin was lifted up before I could finish and I was forced to look at him. Seeing nothing but seriousness within him.

"No you ain't," he retorted, keeping his eyes glued on mine. "You mad I ain't take you to my main crib yet, right?"

I said nothing but he already knew the answer. Two months of seeing each other and it still felt like I hadn't gotten his full trust entirely. And I wanted it. If he saw me as his then didn't I deserve it?

"Can't take you there, Az, 'cause you know what's gon' happen."

I gave him a look of confusion as I waited for him to explain.

He chuckled lightly at my baffled state before letting my chin go. "You know what's gon' happen, Az, quit acting dumb."

"No, Kay, I really don't kno—"

"You do," he said as he cut across my words. "If I take you over there, I'm gonna fuck you."

I instantly froze and remained silent, feeling stupid all of a sudden for not remembering that we were yet to have sex. I mean, sure it was on my mind but it wasn't really a priority, which was weird because he was fine as hell. I had other shit to think about and that included getting to know him even better. Sex was important but it wasn't that important. Or was it? I didn't even know if it was because I hadn't had sex in a while, so I was mostly on the thought that sex was overrated.

"If I take you over to my main spot, I'm gonna fuck the shit outta you. To the point that you won't be able to stand for a couple days," he explained in a tone that sounded comical, yet, still focused and serious at the same time. He was toying and teasing and he knew it.

"Okay," I meekly replied, unsure of what to really do or say.

"And I'm not ready to do that yet, Az, 'cause I know once we bring sex into this," he pointed from me to him, "things are going to get even more deeper."

Then I watched as he shifted out his spot and leaned in closer to me, until our foreheads were almost touching. I could smell his masculine scent and it was low-key starting to drive me wild. Who I was trying to kid? It definitely was starting to drive me wild.

"Just have faith in me," he requested. "Do you have faith in me?"

I simply nodded and observed as he dipped his head closer to me so that our lips could lightly touch. Then our heated kiss began and I was reminded of how much of a good kisser Kaylen was. He knew exactly what to do with that tongue in order to seduce me and as much as I hated it, I couldn't help but love it. Our tongues were circling and playing around with each other for a good ten minutes before Kaylen stopped.

When he got up, headed to his bathroom with his hand on the middle of his basketball shorts, I knew what was up. He didn't even need to speak, I just knew. So while he handled his business, I browsed my phone, dismissing any incoming messages from Michael, and putting my phone on do not disturb. I knew that trying to avoid Michael was never going to work, so I was going to have to face him again sooner or later. But what do I even tell him?

Being a child care worker was fun and all but it wasn't earning me enough and I needed a change of scenery. Even if I told him that, he wouldn't believe it. And he would keep trying to find connections to our relationship and me leaving. As much as I loved him before, I hated how quickly he could make situations seem only about him. That's just what he liked to do.

Once locking off my phone and contemplating on how I was

going to get Michael to back off for good, I was drawn to the flashy screen of Kaylen's iPhone, laying on the recliner next to me. I wasn't one for creeping around on a man's phone but the caller ID on his screen had me tight all of a sudden.

Big Booty Kate.

She was calling him and a few seconds later his phone stopped flashing and went blank. Only for it to suddenly chime in with a text notification, from *Big Booty Kate*. Seeing that she was texting him, my nosiness kicked in and I had to see who this was. He was claiming me as his girl but messing with another chick.

Big Booty Kate: *Miss you Kay.*

Big Booty Kate: *We still have unfinished business from the other week.*

Big Booty Kate: *You can slide through tonight if you like?*

I didn't think that I would get extremely angry but I was. Angry to the point that I wanted to fuck Kaylen up, but I knew better. So I got up, picked up my bag, and got ready to leave. Funny thing was, Kaylen was the one that brought me here, so he was the one that had to take me back. Unless I got an Uber but that would take a while to get here.

When Kaylen got back into the room, he noticed that I was standing up and had a pissed look on my face but didn't say nothing. Instead, he sauntered right up to me and attempted to wrap his arms around me.

"I want to go home now, Kaylen," I snapped, stepping away from him.

"What, why?"

"It's not up for discussion," I said, turning around and walking away from him. "Can we just go?"

"You must be dumb as hell if you think I'm taking you anywhere without talkin' to me first."

"And you must be dumb as hell for sneaking around with chicks behind my back," I yelled, turning around to face him in my stance.

"What you talkin' 'bout?"

"And look who's acting dumb now?" I asked him smugly, not impressed by this act he was trying to put on. "You didn't go see big booty Kate last week?"

He didn't bother responding after that and I knew that everything I had assumed was true. He was claiming me to be his girl but fucking around. It didn't matter who the hell he was, how much clout he had on the streets, that shit just wasn't going to run with me.

"Just take me home," I ordered, placing my hands on my hips confidently.

"No," he replied simply. "I ain't taking you anywhere."

"Are you outta your damn mind? I don't want to be here an—"

"I've already warned you once about that mouth, Az," he reminded me while pointing at me. "Don't make me have to warn you again."

"You really are a fool if you think after today you'll be warning me about anything! You're a cheater! I don't fuck with cheaters."

"Yo, who the hell even told you to go scrolling through my phone?" he rudely questioned, stepping closer to me. His face scrunched up into a tight ball and a frown upon his juicy lips. He was growing angry but I didn't care. He wasn't the one that had any right to get angry, I did. "You shoulda been knowing that going through a nigga's phone is a violation. Scrolling through my phone means you gon' end up finding some shit you ain't gonna like. Matter fact, I should fuck you up for being sneaky," he warned me with no remorse.

"I never scrolled through your phone, I saw her name pop up when she was calling and her texts. You have no right to be angry, Kaylen! I do! I'm the one you've cheated on."

His face softened slightly. "I didn't fuck her if that's what you pissed about."

"So why is she calling you and texting you about some unfinished business then?"

He reluctantly broke eye contact with me before scratching the back of his head. A thing I knew he did when he was nervous. Whatever he was about to say, I knew I wasn't going to like.

"She gave a nigga head one night and that was... Azryah, that was it, I promise you! Az!"

By now, I had ignored his words and walked out his living room, across his front foyer, and left his crib. I didn't want to hear any of the stupid bullshit that had come out and was continuing to come out his mouth. I requested an Uber to my location and thankfully it was nine minutes away. I could wait.

"Az! Yo, can you just listen to me? Az!" he shouted, running towards where I was standing at the front of his open garden, waiting for my Uber. I had my arms crossed and my face facing the road. I was just going to have to block him out.

"Az! I swear that's all it was, I didn't fuck her! How could I fuck her when all I think about is fucking you?"

This stupid, mothafucking pathological liar. He clearly wasn't only thinking about fucking me if he was letting the next bitch suck on him. What sense did that make? I didn't even trust that he hadn't had sex with her.

"I can't believe you're really gonna act like one childish idiot right now," he insulted me and that definitely struck a chord.

"I'm a childish idiot?!" I shrieked at him. "I'm the childish one for being angry that I was cheated on? You really are one stupid mothafucker. We're over, so lose my number, Kaylen, I'm no longer building anything with yo—"

It was as if a switch went off in his head and he no longer became the Kaylen that I had experienced all these past couple of months. He just instantly transformed before my eyes. He tightly grabbed my arm, pulling me close to him, and refusing to let me go.

"Kaylen, what the hell? Let go of m—"

"I told you before about that fuckin' mouth, Azryah, but you just don't fuckin' listen," he said through gritted teeth, hurting me with the way he was gripping my arm. "Quit fucking playing with a nigga, I've told you I didn't fuck her! It was one fuckin' night and she meant nothing to me! You ain't leaving me because I'll kill you before that ever happens and I'm not lying!"

"Get off me, you psyc—"

He instantly pushed me. Pushed me so hard that I ended up falling onto the concrete floor and hearing my phone screen crack too. It had fell out my right hand. I looked up in fear at the tall figure towering over me and glaring down at me with nothing but fury and outrage radiating off him. I could see it in his eyes, he had snapped. Snapped into that ruthless Kaylen that I had been thinking about earlier. He had a look in his eyes like he wanted to kill me. His jaw was tight and twitching.

My eyes became watery when I saw his fists clench and I quietly sighed with disappointment. He was exactly like I had heard. Crazy, demented, and dangerous. But within a second, it was as if another switch had gone off in his head. His face became distraught and his hands unclenched.

"Az," he barely made out above a whisper. "Az, I'm so sorry, baby... I didn't... Fuck, baby, I didn't mean to say that. I didn't mean... to hurt you."

But he had and here we were. He had threatened to kill me and put his hands on me in a painful, intimidating way. I needed to get the hell away from this guy. It was as if my prayers had been answered because my Uber appeared in the drive away and I began to get up.

"Don't touch me," I warned him in a disgusted voice, seeing him try to help me up.

I picked up my phone and gave him a mean, evil mug before walking away from him. He needed to stay the hell away from me.

Me: Az... please just let a nigga explain.

Me: Can you just pick up the phone, please pick up the phone.

Me: So you send me straight to voicemail and refuse to hear me out? Fuck you then!

Me: I take that back baby but please just hear me out.

Me: Azryah! I'm sorry. What the fuck do I need to do to make shit better just tell me?

Me: I don't wanna lose you.

Me: Please.

Me: Yo, answer me soon or I'll come get you and make you listen to me.

Me: Fuckin' try me.

Me: Just hear me out Az... please, a nigga's sorry.

***

"What else am I supposed to do other than give her some space?" I asked Khian in a depressed tone. "She's not picking up a nigga's calls or anything. She doesn't want anything to do with me anymore."

"Can you really blame her though?"

I couldn't lie and say that I didn't blame Azryah for not wanting to fuck with a nigga no more but shit, there was no way that I was going to let her leave my life now. Not now that I had developed some deep, serious feelings for her. Feelings that I knew were only growing more stronger and stronger each day. Especially after what had happened between us.

"It was an accident. I been warned her about that damn mouth though. She knew not to fuck with me," I explained with a shrug.

"I thought you didn't mind your females talkin' to you crazy," Khian amusingly said. "Don't that shit make you hard or something?"

"Yeah, but she's not just any female," I reminded him. "She's my girl, I need some level of respect because of how loyal I'm being to her."

Khian immediately began to deeply laugh at me, unable to contain himself for a few seconds before piping up, "Yo, you're talking shit right now. You just mad she's confident enough to keep coming at you. I can agree a female's mouth sometimes just makes you wanna put your hands on her but I can't lie and say it ain't sexy when a female can stand her own."

I rolled my eyes at him before covering my forehead with my palm, sighing in defeat.

"All I want is for her to pick up my calls and let me explain. I'm going crazy without her man," I fumed. "Why she gotta be so fucking stubborn?"

"Nigga, I know you're quickly falling in love and shit, but you really need to chill. You were the one that put your hands on her, so you just need to give her all the space she needs, you can't keep forcing her to listen to you. You've apologized once just let her be the one to contact you," Khian advised calmly, before reaching into his front glove compartment and pulling out a small plastic container. "But anyways, here's the shit you asked for. Don't overdo it, bro. You only need one and he's gone."

I removed my hand from my forehead and looked ahead with curiosity at my brother. I reached for the container out his hand and examined the three tiny, white pills sitting comfortably in the corner. Times like these was when Khian being a medically licensed doctor came in handy, indeed.

"Why'd you give me three if only one will do the job?" I asked with a smirk. He already knew I was one to overdo things and here he was, giving me more than needed.

"'Cause unfortunately, I know your ass like the back of my hand but I'm just letting you know that one will do the job."

"One might do the job, but three gon' do it even better. It's been a minute since I've been needing to get rid of this stupid ass nigga and this is just the perfect way for me to that," I stated boldly. "Latisha's gonna slip it in his drink and we're good to go, ain't no more mothafuckin' Jer—"

"Nigga," Khian interrupted me abruptly, "Ain't no we when it comes to this, I been told you. It's all you. I'm just indiscreetly leading you to a simple, clean way to get rid of your enemies without needing to get actual blood on your hands. But absolutely no traces back to me, bro. I swear on everything, if this gets back on me and I lose my licen—"

"Bro, chill," I cut him off, irritated with the fact that he would think I would let him get caught. "We brothers, and I ain't never gon' let that shit happen. 'Preciate you for looking out for me though. You know how much problems I've had with this nigga about territory over Brooklyn already. As soon as he's gone, it's all mine."

"And with that comes big responsibility, you know that, right?" he seriously queried, raising his brow at me. "Shit's only gonna get harder 'cause it means more eyes on you and more niggas waiting for you to fuck up so they can steal that spot."

"I'm good, Khi," I promised. "You ain't gotta worry about me not being ready 'cause I'ma be just fine. I've got this shit under control 100%."

"I hope you ain't told Azryah about your shit?"

"Nah... but obviously, she had an idea of what I do already before getting involved with me," I reminded him.

"But are you planning to tell her anything more? About you moving weight in Brooklyn and expanding? All the guns and the narc—"

"Not right now, no, bro," I said, wanting to stop his worries. "I ain't even sure if I can fully trust her with all that information yet. It's all only been a couple of months and she still ain't talking to a nigga, so we'll just see. If it's possible, I'm hoping that she never finds out the full extent of the shit I do."

"Why?" Khian suspiciously asked. "You scared she's gonna run to the cops?"

"Nah, she knows damn well not to do all that. I already threatened to kill her ass once and she knew I was dead serious about it, so she wouldn't try that foul shit. I'm worried it's gonna ruin shit. She'll constantly be cautious about what I do, become one of those chicks in

119

those dumb ass urban fiction shits and pressure me to leave the game. But how am I supposed to leave something that I love? Something that I'm addicted to? That shit just don't make no sense to me."

Khian grinned while saying, "Well damn, nigga, I ain't even know your ass reads. Could read to be exact."

"Yeah, shut your ass up, yo," I snapped. "I don't. But one of them bitches I was fucking with before Azryah was yapping some shit about some drug dealer called Blaze and his wifey wanting him to get out the game... basically some bullshit fairy tale shit, and I automatically knew from then that letting my bitch know everything about what I do and how I do wouldn't sit right with me. Except if I really, really, really loved her ass."

"You falling for her ain't you? Who's to say you won't fall in love with her really, really, really deeply?"

"Man, I don't know, if I do then I do. But right now, I gotta get her off my mind and focus on getting rid of this nigga. Like you said, giving her some space is key, right? Then that's just what I gotta do," I voiced tensely, trying to convince myself more than him. The only thing I wanted to do now was take my ass 'round to Azryah's, kidnap her away, and force her to listen to what I had to say. Including making her promise to never leave me like that ever again. I wanted to do all of that without laying a single finger on her. Crazy shit, right?

But for now, I had work to focus on. I needed to get rid of Jermaine and life would be Gucci. I was already in charge of most dope gangs and dope spots in Brooklyn. And if I wasn't in charge in terms of leadership, then I was the one that their leaders were coming to for the good shit. In simple terms, I was the plug. And I moved weight with my dope boys through the streets of Brooklyn. It wasn't easy taking niggas spot at first but quickly, I became skilled at it and here I was today.

Azryah not talking to me was now officially on the bottom of my list. I really didn't need the stress that thinking about her had brought me lately. I had real shit to stress about and worrying about some bitch just wasn't gonna work.

Only thing was, Azryah wasn't just some bitch. She was my girlfriend. I didn't care about what had happened, we were still together. We may have been taking a short break for her to forgive me but that's all it was. If I caught her with any other dude or doing some foul shit that she knew I wouldn't like, then on God, I was going to kill her.

***

"Give me one good reason why I shouldn't pull this mothafuckin' trigga right now? Huh? Say something, nigga!"

I usually wasn't one to start shooting up niggas in their damn apartments but with the confirmation from Latisha, that Jermaine was dead and the pictures to prove that shit, I was more than ready to takeover. Me taking over, included going to pay the one nigga that refused to do any business with me. He was Jermaine's ole boy, Trent, who had always had it out for me ever since I started communicating with his boss. Honestly, I knew he was the main reason for why Jermaine didn't wanna work with me. He had poisoned him with lies about me.

Now his boss was dead, however and I was the new boss. He was defenseless and alone. So what could he do other than beg?

"K-Kaylen, man, p-please," he stuttered shakily. "Shit was a mistake, I shoulda trusted you."

Boogie immediately let out a loud laugh behind me. "Funny how he says that now he's got a nine to his face. Dumb mothafucka."

I couldn't help but follow suit and laugh alongside my goon. It was true though. Trent had always tried to come across as tough and hard headed to me, the boy had even tried to fight me once but Jermaine calmed him down real quick. Fuck a fight, they both knew I really wasn't one to be played with. I'm sending bullets into niggas hearts not punches. That's not the way I roll.

"P-Please, Kaylen," Trent begged, tears rolling down the side of his face as he stared up at me. "Don't kill me, man. I'll do anything! I'll work for you!"

"Work for me?" I questioned him with a glad smile. "Unfortunately, I don't work with rats that talk hella shit about me behind my back." I cocked the gun as I pressed it harder against his sweaty forehead. "Night night, nigga."

Bang! Bang!

Once I had blown his brains out, all over his carpeted rug, the three things on my mind was telling Boogie to get the clean-up crew down here and get me a new t-shirt. And whipping my phone out to see the two missed calls and messages from Azryah. Unfortunately, only two of those things happened and it didn't involve any calls or texts from the girl I couldn't stop thinking about. I stared down at my bright screen with disdain.

She had my mind corrupted and I wasn't liking it. Things didn't sit right with me knowing that this one female was mind fucking me. I wanted to stop thinking about her but I couldn't. I wanted to stop dreaming about her but I couldn't. And the dreams were much worse than they originally were when I had first seen her dancing at Club Onyx. Much worse.

What did I need to do to get her out of my head?

~ *Michael* ~

"So they just found him poisoned?"

"Yeah, the toxicology report found a high concentration of potassium cyanide in his drink," my partner, Lenny, responded. "It appears to be suicide."

But I knew, without a doubt, that suicide had nothing to do with this situation.

"And what about his worker, Trent?"

"He's still missing, his girlfriend is unable to get into contact with him."

"You know Kaylen Walker's responsible for all of this right?"

"I know that, Mike, but you and I can't prove shit right now. So let's just keep our heads down and look for evidence."

This shit was annoying.

Highly annoying. Why was this dude getting away with serious crime in this city? I just wanted to make sure that he spent the rest of his life in a jail cell because I couldn't sleep well at night knowing he was a free man. He was dangerous and a notorious criminal. He needed to be locked up and kept away from society because he was a threat to anyone. He had too much clout on the streets and it really irritated me. I needed him behind bars. No one in this stupid department was willing to go through the risks I was in order to get Kaylen Walker in jail. It's as if he had them under his own spell.

I wouldn't be surprised if most of these cops were being bribed by him because they weren't as determined and enthusiastic as me when it came to working on this case and getting Kaylen in jail, permanently. They were always slow with paperwork and just downright lazy. None of them wanted him in jail as bad as I wanted him. He needed to rot away for life.

I hated drug dealers. They caused too much problems in communities and believed that everything was rightfully theirs when it was not. They were selfish, violent, and murderers. Back in Chicago, I had dealt with many and made sure that majority of the top dogs were sitting in a cold jail cell right now. I needed to make sure that became a reality for Kaylen because there was no way that I could allow him to keep on living on the streets of Brooklyn. It was time for him to go.

I knew that Kaylen was behind Jermaine dying and Trent turning up missing. I also knew his reasons. With Jermaine out the way, Kaylen could easily claim Jermaine's remaining territory in Brooklyn and finally have power to move all the product he wanted to. It didn't matter how smart and quick Kaylen appeared to be, I could see straight past him. And I was going to spend the rest of my life making sure that he spent the rest of his life in a jail cell.

Without a doubt.

~ *Khian* ~

I mean what else could I say?

My brother was falling in love with this chick. Without a doubt, Azryah belonged to Kaylen.

Despite the issues they were having due to Kaylen's temper, I knew one way or another they were going to get past it. Kaylen had a temper on him, quite frankly, we both did but when it came to loving females - a thing we rarely did, we took that shit seriously. Kaylen was falling for Azryah, so he most definitely wasn't going to let her go. There was no doubt in my mind about it.

Things would work themselves out and Azryah would be running back to him. Kaylen always had a hold on females and I expected Azryah to be no different. It was only going to be a matter of time before she never wanted to let him go and not the other way 'round. Right now, I was heading to Michelle's. I had flexed with her last weekend but a nigga was experiencing withdrawal symptoms from being away from her for just a couple of days. I needed to see her, have her in my arms for a bit before I fucked her. Besides, I did enjoy her company and she definitely knew that. She was the only female I was bothered to make an effort to see these days. As a doctor I was busy 24/7, but on my days off, there was only one face I wanted to see and one box I wanted to slide into.

Hers.

Once parking my car in Michelle's apartment parking lot, I contemplated about Kaylen and his little situation that I had helped him sort out. Yes, I helped Kaylen kill niggas. Was I ashamed of it? Yes. Did I regret it? No. I knew it was for a good cause. The cause of ensuring my brother stayed protected while being involved in this street shit. He was my twin and I was always going to have his best interests at heart. No matter what. Was there a possibility that I could get caught supplying my brother with toxins? Yes, there was but that possibility was low because I was extremely careful. I wasn't about to get caught anytime soon. Ever to be honest with you.

Ten minutes later, I was standing outside Michelle's front door and reaching into my back pocket for my key. Yeah, that's right. Michelle had decided to give me a key. She said it was because opening up the door for me when I was always coming around was daunting. So she gave me her spare key and now, I could walk up into her apartment whenever I felt like it. Even to the point that if she wasn't home, I could stay and crash for a bit while waiting for her to get back.

Of course, I was aware that Azryah lived with her but we hardly saw each other. It wasn't like I had made it my duty to stay away from her but it wasn't my duty to go looking for her either.

Upon entering, I slipped off my Jordans and headed to the kitchen to get a glass of water. I knew Michelle was out right now running errands and shit, but I wasn't stressing. I would simply wait in her bedroom and get busy with her when she arrived.

Arriving in the kitchen was a slight surprise for me because I quickly laid eyes on Azryah. She was sitting on the kitchen counter, staring down at her phone. But when I entered, her head shot up.

"Oh hey," she greeted me shyly.

"'Sup, Azryah," I responded in a friendly tone, walking towards her. I didn't expect her to get down from the counter but she had and when I was in front of her, she sauntered closer. She was sporting tight grey shorts, a black crop top, and those black puma fur slides that girls went crazy over.

"Nice to see you," she said as she walked into my arms and I had no choice but to friendly hug her back.

"Nice to see you too," I stated coolly before adding, "I'm sure Kaylen would love to see you."

She rolled her eyes in annoyance before attempting to turn away and walk out the kitchen. However, I grabbed her arm, stopping her from leaving. She looked down with surprise at my hand then shrugged me off.

"Look, Azryah, he didn't send me to talk to you but he's my twin and I'll always do what's best for him. I know he hurt you but you must know he didn't mean that shit."

"Oh, so he didn't mean to threaten to kill me?"

"Nah, he definitely meant that shit," I voiced boldly, making her mouth drop open. "I meant him putting his hands on you, pushing you."

"He meant all of it," she affirmed, staring up at me with hostility. "I don't want to be around that type of guy."

"That type of guy is the one that really cares about you though and is bound to make sure nothing happens to you when you're with him."

"But something could happen to me while I'm with him," she counter argued. "He could attack me worse this time or even better, kill me."

I simply sighed at her, coming to the realization that she was just as stubborn as Kaylen had said she was.

"A'ight, Azryah, I'm not gonna press you about Kay anymore. Just know, he's sorry and didn't mean that shit," I concluded as I turned to walk towards the fridge.

"You wouldn't treat me like that, would you, Khian?" she questioned me. Her innocent, curious tone making me stop in my tracks of getting to the fridge.

"I mean, I can't lie we both have a temper, but we would never physically beat the shit out of you or any female," I explained, eyeing her closely.

"So, you would threaten to kill me if I tried to leave you?"

I couldn't lie, all her questioning was becoming dangerous. I didn't want to say the wrong thing to her and make her get the wrong idea about me. I also didn't want to come across as being too strong.

"The girl I'm with, is probably someone I see myself marrying, someone I'm going to start a future with, an empire... someone I'm falling in love with. Threatening to kill you would make me crazy but it's only because I'm crazy over you. Crazy over every little thing that you do and crazy over how you make me feel. When I'm loving you, I'm only loving you and I expect the same. Crazy niggas love the hardest and that's just the way shit is," I announced truthfully and looked on to see if I could tell what she was thinking and how she was feeling. She only had a slight smile on her lips though.

"Well, damn," she began. "Michelle is one lucky girl then."

"Michelle?"

"Yeah, your girlfriend," she told me with a smirk.

I gave her a strange look, "Michelle ain't my girl. We're jus—"

"Just fucking, I know but the rate you're going, she'll be your girl."

"I'm not really looking for a girl right now. I'm a busy guy and I'm just tryna live my life," I stated confidently.

"Anything could happen," she lightly sang. "But as for Kay and me, who knows? I really just need some space away from him."

"You do know he's never gonna leave you alone, right?"

"I know," she mumbled quietly. "That's the thing that's driving me crazy the most."

"I think you should just hear him out, but at the end of the day, it's still your choice; just know that whatever you decide doesn't matter. My twin likes you, badly, and he's making no attempts on letting you walk out his life anytime soon."

She simply nodded before announcing, "Again, it was nice seeing you, Khian," she said. "You know... for a while I thought you didn't like me."

If that had been true then Kaylen woulda fucked her by now and kept it moving. "Nah, I do like you, Azryah."

"You do?"

"Yeah, girl," I assured her. "I fuck with you."

"Alrightie," she concluded, waving shyly at me before leaving the kitchen.

I must have missed hearing the front door open because just as Azryah walked out the kitchen, Michelle popped up in a few quick seconds later.

"Hey, sexy," I greeted her with my arms crossed against my chest, closely watching her walk towards me. She said nothing but I didn't need to hear words come out her mouth to know that she was pissed off. She had a scowl growing on her pretty face. What the hell was wrong with her?

"Mich, what's wrong?"

"...Nothing."

"Okay."

"Oh, so now you don't care about me?"

What. The. Actual. Fuck?

"What the fuck is wrong with you? I just asked you what was wrong and you said nothing," I reminded her sternly. "Now you're acting like I don't care about you."

Michelle said nothing and kept quiet. She had a miserable facial expression on her face and I wasn't liking it. So, I pulled her by her arms, bringing her closer towards me. "Mich, what's wrong?"

"...It's that time of the month," she mumbled. Now that explained her strange behavior and I understood completely what was going on. I was also low-key depressed about the fact that we weren't going to be able to smash tonight or for the next couple days.

"Oh damn," I voiced gently, lifting her chin up so I could peck her lips. "It's cool though, we can just cuddle tonight. You tell me whatever you need and I got you, girl."

She beamed up at me happily and nodded. At least now, I knew that there was no beef between us. I really didn't need no problems between us.

CHAPTER 7

~ *Kaylen* ~

*I*t had all been CJ's idea.

I didn't even feel like going out. But a nigga was bored and needed something to take my mind off Azryah. She still wasn't trying to get in contact with me after I had decided to chill on pestering her with calls. Now, I wished I hadn't done that bullshit because I felt hopeless and worthless.

"Just relax, man, she gon' come 'round soon enough," CJ stated cheerfully while pressing hard on my left shoulder. "In the meantime, just enjoy this night out away from her and your goons. We just finna have a good time tonight!"

CJ was a guy that rarely attended strip clubs, so for my cousin to be attending Club Onyx on my behalf, showed how much he cared. He was really trying to get me in better spirits. Believe me, I had been in one absolute disgusting mood and I really didn't see myself getting out of it anytime soon. However, when CJ requested for a stripper to come give me a quick lap dance, my mood heightened slightly.

Shorty was bad indeed. Red bone, curvy, and had a talented way of grinding her ass on my dick. She had a wild look in those maroon eyes of hers, telling me that she wanted me. I was even considering taking her home with me tonight. I couldn't even remember the last time I had actually been able to dive into some pussy. It felt like it had been years, even though, I knew it had only really been a few months now. All because of Azryah.

Man, what the hell did I need to do to forget about her? But forgetting about her was most definitely not an option. It wasn't even something I could try to do because she had won me too deep. I was falling for her badly. Even more badly now that we were apart.

While I continued to slightly enjoy the lap dance from shorty on my lap, CJ seemed to be focused on the main performance stage. In total, there were four silver poles along a row and each one had a dancer about to start her dancing. I couldn't make out any of their faces yet because the stage lights were blacked out. But when the lights came on, I swear I instantly lost it. All sense of calm went flying out the window. Completely out.

I didn't even need to see her pretty face properly to know that she was there. I could spot that body from a mile away. The situation definitely wasn't being helped because of the fact that she was practically naked. Wearing nothing but a thin red G-string in between her legs and a matching mesh bralette. The mesh that could allow every single thirsty male up in this club to feast their eyes upon her breasts. Shit that was only for my eyes to see.

I really couldn't believe this shit.

The half-naked dancer on my lap was still eagerly trying to please me, but I only grew irritated and pushed her off me, paying her protests no mind once she had hit the floor. Seeing Azryah on the stage and beginning to dance, only heightened my frustration.

"Yo, Kay... don't make a scene man, just wait 'til she's finished."

Finished? CJ must have forgotten what type of man I was. I didn't wait for no one to finish. I just did things on my own accord and that's just the way it was.

"I'ma see you later, CJ," I fumed through gritted teeth. My fists were clenched and I was already out my seat. Seeing the way Azryah was freely dancing for a crowd of thirsty ass men, throwing winks and lip bites their way, had me tight. I didn't even bother hesitating, I stormed out of my seat and headed towards the main stage.

I pushed aggressively through the crowd of males, throwing menacing looks their way. They knew best not to try me though. Everyone knew who the hell I was. I looked up at the stage, seeing Azryah twirl around on her pole before coming to a halt when her eyes landed on mine.

The fear in her eyes was more than enough to let me know that she was fully aware of how much trouble she was in.

"Get your ass down from that stage," I yelled to her above the loud, booming music. Seeing that she wasn't making any attempts to move, I decided to yell again. "Now!"

She instantly jumped up at my last shout and decided to move towards the side exit but I stopped her.

"Get your dumb ass down from that stage and over here right

now," I snapped at her.

She turned to face me and threw me a bewildered look before stating, "But, Kaylen, I need to cha-"

"Shut the fuck up," I berated her. "Get over here. I ain't gon' tell you again. You want me to fuck you up in front of all these people? Let's go!"

She didn't bother disobeying me this time or try to argue with me. She just sauntered to the edge of the stage before sitting down and jumping off. By now, I had taken off my leather jacket and was holding it up for her to grab. She avoided eye contact with me but still took it. Then while she placed it on, I mean mugged the crowd looking at us both before leading the way to the nearest exit.

Five minutes later, we were outside my Maserati. I unlocked it and got in, too angry to be a gentleman to Azryah and open the car door for her like I usually did. When she got in beside me, instead of yelling at her like I really wanted to, I turned on my car engine and began to drive out Club Onyx's parking lot.

"Kaylen, where are you taking me?"

I didn't bother answering her. I was still too pissed off with what she had done. I didn't even think answering her was a good idea right now because it was only going to lead to me saying some extra rude shit to her ass. It was just best I kept quiet.

"Kaylen, I asked you a question."

And can't you see that I'm really not in the mood to answer your ass right now? Didn't she realize how angry she had gotten me? After she had promised to never strip ever again. She didn't need to strip ever again. So why the hell had she done that shit? Knowing fully well that her stripping was going to get me mad. This had to be revenge for me hurting her. Yeah, that's exactly what this bullshit was. Revenge.

"Kaylen!"

"Didn't I already tell your ass to shut the fuck up? You want me to make you do that shit?" I fired back at her, not bothering to look at her. I didn't want to look at her because I was afraid of her seeing the look in my eyes. The look that probably read, *I want to kill your pretty ass for disrespecting me like that tonight, Azryah. But then again, I don't want to kill you. I'd rather just fuck the shit out of you and make sure you never forget to never disrespect a nigga like that again.*

"Kaylen, take me home."

"I will do no such thing."

She huffed in frustration. "We're not together. You have no right to be forcing me out of my work place."

"Your workplace? Your workplace or the place you can dress half naked in, looking like a little hoe."

"Take me home!" she cried. "Now!"

"You screaming and shouting as if that's about to make any difference. Matter fact, fuck you, Azryah! Fuck your feelings! I give you space and you decide to go back to stripping. I told you I was gonna provide for you, look after you, and you resort back to the one thing I told you not to do no more."

"You're not the boss of me, you're not my boyfriend, you're not breaking my back out every night, so no I don't answer to you. Never have and never will!"

"So a nigga gotta start breaking your back out every night for you to listen to me?" I asked her with a sly smirk.

She groaned in disgust before responding, "You hurt me. Threatened to kill me and you expect me to be okay with that?"

I kept my eyes on the road as I continued to drive to our destination. "And I'ma still threaten to kill your ass, even after what happened. I think you might have forgotten what type of nigga you fuckin' with."

"I'm not fucking with any type of nigga," she retorted. "Because you're taking my ass straight home."

"A'ight, bet," I concluded simply and deciding to keep quiet.

She didn't bother striking up a conversation with me and I was cool with it. One thing I knew from the second I laid eyes on her was that I definitely wasn't taking her home. I was taking her to my crib and once she realized that, she was going to finally comprehend what was going down between us tonight. Comprehend was an understatement, though. Because as soon as she laid eyes on the golden gates, I had pulled up to, she quietly gasped.

"Kay…Kay, stop."

I didn't even bother looking at her face. I rolled my car window down so that I could punch in the code to my house gates.

"Kaylen, please… don't."

Again, I ignored her as I pressed in my code and watched my gates open. At least, now she had gotten the picture.

"Kay," she pleaded, reaching for my arm. I lightly shook her arm off so that I could continue to drive my car into my front doorway without being distracted by her touch.

"Just relax, Az," I said calmly, sensing her apprehensive tone. "Relax."

Once I had drove into my driveway, I parked by my front lawn and stopped the car. Then I turned to face her, seeing that she had her head down and her eyes on her hands. She was nervous I could tell.

"Az, look nothing that you don't want to happen is gonna happen tonight."

"So why'd you bring me here?"

"To be honest, I don't really know," I truthfully admitted. "All I know is that a nigga was so mad at seeing you half naked on that stage, and I just wanted to snatch you up out of there."

"And now you've snatched me out of there," she fumed, staring up at me suspiciously. "What exactly are your intentions?"

"I don't know."

"You do."

She was dead ass right. I most definitely knew. "Look, Azryah... All I really know is that I like you a lot. I can't seem to get you out of my mind. I'm sorry about pushing you, I'm sorry I threatened to kill you but me threatening to kill you is just something you have to get used to." She threw me a crazy look. "Because it's my way of expressing how much I like you. I like you so much that I don't want any niggas liking you and looking at you the same way that I do. Because if they do and you were to give one your attention, I'd kill him first, make you watch, and then kill you. And that's just the way I am. I'm crazy, protective, and dominant over mine. And I don't care what you say, Az, you and I both know that you're mine. Now you can decide what happens here tonight, I don't mind taking you home, but I'd rather you stay with a nigga tonight. We ain't really gotta do shit but talk and chill. I just want you and I to be cool again. Most importantly, I want you in my arms tonight."

I eyed her closely, expecting her to say something smart back to me. But instead of speaking, she had a sexy smile growing on her lips, and I could tell that she had finally forgiven a nigga.

"Az?"

Instead of responding to me, she moved out her seat, kept her eyes on mine, before leaning her head closer to mine.

"Yeah?" she queried in a low, sensual whisper.

"What do you wanna do?"

"I don't mind," she simply answered.

I couldn't help but chuckle at her mood change. This was the same chick that had wanted me to take her home a few minutes ago.

"Are you sure?" I questioned her seriously. If she didn't mind then that meant that whatever was going down to tonight was based on my choice. And I really only had one idea in my mind. The idea I had from the very moment I laid eyes on her pretty face.

She nodded reassuringly before dipping her lips to hover above mine before pecking them gently. It was a quick, sweet peck that definitely left me wanting more. Our foreheads instantly touched and I looked down, only to realize how sexy she looked in her stripper outfit.

I had been too angry with her when I first got a glimpse of her, but now I could see everything perfectly. Her nipples looked hard as fuck and I could feel myself hardening in my pants as I imagined my fingers toying and playing with her buds. Or better yet, using my tongue to swirl around her nipples and play around with her fat, succulent tits.

Before I could even realize, Azryah had moved her forehead off mine and positioned her head in the crook of my neck.

"Shit, Az...."

Things happened so quickly. It was as if I had suddenly snapped my fingers so that Azryah had turned into a completely new person. She was now tenderly sucking and kissing on my neck, like a true freak. I had always known that, that freaky nature of Azryah's was hidden deep, I just had to be the one to uncover it and tonight, I was doing just that.

My hands quickly grabbed onto my jacket that she was wearing and pulled it down her arms and off her body. Then, I got the opportunity to grab her breasts and gently massage them, all while she was making sweet love to my neck.

It didn't take long for things to turn wild, drastically. Shit was too heated between us and the urge to fuck each other had strongly built up. We couldn't even get away from the car and head into my crib.

So I fucked her in missionary, on my Maserati's car hood.

"Oh my... Oh my God, Kaylen!"

This had to be the wildest shit I had ever done with a chick. I considered my cars to be extremely valuable items, kept them spotless with not a single scratch or damaged paint job in sight. No one was allowed to touch my shit except me or my mechanics.

Now here I was, trousers and boxers down to my ankles. Casually having sex on my car. Something that I had never actually considered in this lifetime but Azryah was bringing out a whole other freaky side of me. I was already aware of how much of a freak I was, but my freak status had gone up another level.

"Az, damn it… you got me weak, fuck," I groaned as I thrusted deep into her tightness.

There was only one word I could use to describe how her pussy felt around my dick. Heaven. Out of all the girls I had ever been with, not one of them had made me feel this way. None of them had me blushing or feeling butterflies grow in my stomach. To make matters worse, I wasn't wearing a rubber. Every squeeze and sensation coming from her pussy I could feel intensely. I wasn't trying to get her pregnant, so I knew I was going to have to pull out when my climax came near.

Our bodies continued to rock in time together against my car, as I kept pounding into her. Even my car was lightly shaking against both our bodies.

"Uhhh, Kay… slow down."

"No," I half whispered and half groaned.

Seeing the way her eyes were rolling to the back of her head as I buried my dick harder and faster into her, had me grinning. She was telling me to slow down when she knew, damn well, she was enjoying this shit just as much as me.

"Kay... I can't, agh! I can't... I can't take it all."

"You can and you will," I demanded, deeply exhaling as I pulled out her wet box and then pushed right back in. Keeping a consistent, fast pace and ensuring her legs weren't sliding off my waist. But I wasn't happy with keeping her legs around my waist, so I had to lift them both up onto my shoulders, stroking her warm thighs as I fucked her brains out.

Yeah, this was the craziest, hottest sex I had ever had.

I was even more glad that I was having sex on my car hood with no one else but Azryah. I was going to make sure that she never forgot this night and the many other nights to come between us. I was never letting her go now that I knew about the true extent of the treasure between her thighs.

"Ahhhh... Kay... God!" She moaned louder, taking each rapid push that I made inside her.

"You ain't.... ever goin' to strip ever again," I told her as I rode her, closely observing the looks of pleasure sweeping across her beautiful face. I knew any minute now, she was going to cum and as bad as I wanted to myself, I needed to make sure that she got hers first. Her getting her nut would always be the most important thing to me. "Ain't that right, Azryah?"

She nodded submissively, biting her lips, and whimpering at my dick still moving in and out of her.

"I wanna hear you say that shit," I ordered firmly.

"Uhh… I'm never stripping again."

"You're never leaving me again?"

"I'm never leaving you, agh!"

"And you're going to keep taking all this dick?"

"Mmm," she passionately moaned as my thrusts slowed but became rougher and harder. "I'm going to keep tak… taking all this dick!"

I confidently smirked before lifting her legs off my shoulders and back down to my torso. Then, I leaned down towards where her head lay on my hood, silencing her moans and whimpers with a sensual kiss.

It's crazy the things you could get females to say when they were under the influence of your sex. One thing I knew for sure was, she wasn't going to be able to take back a single word she had just said.

~ *Khian* ~

"So, I just wanna know… what is this?"

And there it was.

After eating her pussy and dicking her down for the past two hours, here she was, standing in the doorway of her bathroom, asking every female's favorite question. This was her opportunity to hear me either claim her or disown her completely.

"Two people who like each other, kicking it," I responded coolly, folding my hands behind my head and keeping a locked gaze on her. Her face remained expressionless and I was unsure how she was feeling by my words.

"Okay… But do you see this going somewhere?"

"We are going somewhere," I replied with a smirk. "We be diving in these sheets almost every night."

"Khi, stop playing. Do you see this going somewhere serious?"

"I mean…"

What could I really say? I was feeling her but that was mostly due to the fact that she was good in bed. I didn't see this going anywhere serious, honestly. I wasn't falling in love with her and I didn't think I would ever end up falling in love with her. But that didn't change the fact that I liked her. Last time we had messed around, she became too much to handle. But now, we were on agreeable terms of us just being fuck buddies. However, she was about to ruin it. I could just feel it.

"I'm not trying to get into a relationship with anyone right now, man," I explained simply. "I'm not ready for it."

"So why are you constantly coming to my place, keeping my company, cooking for me? If you don't want a relationship, why are you putting yourself through this hassle?"

I instantly threw her a strange look, continuing to keep a locked gaze on her now irritated facial expression.

"Yo, where is all of this comin' from?" I asked, rubbing my head down my face. All I really wanted to do was sleep or fuck around again but because of Michelle, now we had to have a conversation on the future of our situation.

There was no future. Point blank period. But I really didn't want to hurt her feelings. I didn't want to crush her because I knew that if I revealed the truth to her, that's exactly what would happen. Her feelings would be hurt.

"I just need to know," she affirmed, not properly answering my question.

"I don't think you should be tryin' to rush things, Mich, it's n—"

"You were the one that started hitting me up in the first place, surely you must know if you want us to get into a relations—"

"First of all," I snapped, interrupting her words with a frown. I knew treating her like she was my girlfriend was going to make her get the wrong idea. I should have never let it get this far. I should have just smashed and kept it moving. "Don't ever cut me off like that again. Secondly, do you want me to leave? 'Cause I can do that if you like and I can be dead ass serious about not hitting you up anymore, if that's what you would like."

Michelle's irritated expression began to soften. I knew she wouldn't want me going anywhere. If she was curious about us starting a relationship together, then she wouldn't want me going anywhere. I wasn't really going anywhere, I just didn't want her asking me stupid questions anymore.

"Khian, no… I don't want you to leave," she stated innocently as she made her way towards the bed. "I just want to know what's going on with us."

"I think you should just be patient," I advised. "Let's just continue to enjoy each other. What's the point of rushing things? You buggin' out right now for no reason at all."

By now, she had made it to my bedside and I reached for her bare thigh before gently throwing her onto the bed. Once she was on, I quickly climbed on top of her, leaning my head down into the nook of her neck.

"But, Khian, I just… mmh, I just want to know."

My lips were now gently kissing on her soft skin. Inhaling the sweet scent of her perfume as I made love to her neck. I just needed to dick her down and make her shut up. I didn't want to talk about any relationships, I just wanted some pussy.

"Khi," she whispered, deeply breathing with anticipation. "Please…. Mmh."

"All you… need to know… is that… I'm about… to beat… that pussy up for the day," I said boldly in between each kiss on her neck.

Before she could even try to protest or say some shit, I lifted my head and sealed our lips together. Pushing past her soft lips so that I could dominate her mouth with tongue.

I knew that the time for Michelle and I to come to an end was nearby. I believed that deep down, she knew that too. And she was just going to have to accept it. I was never going to be her boyfriend, husband, or whatever else she thought.

It was only ever about sex. Not commitment and definitely not love.

~ Michelle ~

I could feel my situation with Khian slipping away and I knew I couldn't allow that to happen. I was in love with him and I know that saying that makes me sound crazy but I really don't care. He means so much to me, and I don't want to lose him to that bitch Azryah. I overheard him speaking to her in our kitchen when I had arrived back home. And when she left, I pretended to be walking through the door and gave her a fake ass smile.

Even though he hadn't said anything about having feelings for her, I just knew he did. I could feel it in my gut and I always believed my gut instincts. Khian had feelings for her. He was able to talk to her so freely and comfortably, so I can only imagine what goes through his mind when he looks at her. I know he wants her. But I can't let that happen because he belongs to me.

I lost him once before but I'm not about to do it again because he means too much to me. I see us building a real future together and Khian being the father of our kids. All three of them. Two boys and one girl. Yeah, I had planned all this shit out already and I was going to make sure that it happened.

I didn't trust Azryah either. She was way too eager to talk to him in the kitchen. It made me wonder about other private conversations they had been having behind my back when I was not around. Given the right opportunity, I knew that Azryah would jump at the chance of having both twins. I didn't trust her at all. Fuck the fact that she was my best friend, if she was fucking Khian behind my back, then I was going to kill her. Without a doubt.

Khian belonged to me only and I just wanted Azryah to focus on her relationship with Kaylen. Honestly, I didn't want to see her happier than me. And these days, it seemed that she was happier than me. I didn't like that. I needed to be the happy one.

"So you don't trust her, even though she's in a relationship with Khian's twin?" my sister, Gabi, asked curiously. "Girl, you really are crazy."

"No, Gabi," I snapped at her through the phone. I know she's sneaking around with him. My gut is telling me. And if she is, then I'm going to have to kill her stupid ass."

"Please tell me you're joking."

"I'm really not, Gabi," I affirmed. "Khian belongs to me."

"Khian belongs to you but yet, he won't claim you? How does that work exactly?"

"He's going to come around eventually, he just needs some motivation and I'll have to be the one to give it to him."

"What exactly did he say when you first asked him?" she queried.

"That we were just kicking it and having a good time. But I'm tired of just kicking it and having a good time. I want more, I deserve more."

"But he doesn't want more," she reminded me, pissing me off.

"Like I said, I just need to give me some motivation and make sure he makes me his girlfriend."

Being in a relationship with Khian was now officially my number one priority. I had to be the only one woman for him. No one else rightfully deserved that spot but me. After all the shit I had done to make him happy, giving him this pussy whenever and wherever he wanted it. He must have been crazy if he thought I was going to let him slip through my fingers.

"You can't force the man to get into a relationship with you, Mich, he has to wan—"

"Are you going to support me or not, sister?" I questioned her, cutting her off abruptly. She was starting to piss me the fuck off.

"No," she commented with a sigh. "I definitely will not. You're crazy."

"Cool. Delete my number then. You're officially dead to me."

"Miche—"

I hung up on her and blocked her number. She may have been my sister but she was linked to me purely by blood. There was no other reason for us to be attached. Besides, she resided in Cali, leaving me in Brooklyn all by myself. I didn't have much friends over here including Azryah, but who needs friends when there's money to be made?

Our father was dead and our mother had been a deadbeat since the day she had us. I hardly spoke to her and now I had just added Gabi to that list. She was younger than me by two years and had always been fine without me. She could go to hell for all I care. She wasn't planning to support me, then I really didn't need her.

Ding!

I looked down at my bright iPhone screen, only to see that a text notification had come in from an unknown number.

Unknown: *Michelle. I need your help. It's Michael.*

I couldn't help but feel confused. I was aware that Michael was Azryah's ex-boyfriend, who was a cop. Why exactly was he texting me right now for help? We were not friends, never had been, and never would be.

Me: *Hi. What's going on? I quickly texted back before saving his number in my contacts list.*

Michael: *I know its been a minute since you heard from me but I really do need your help.*

Me: *With what?*

Michael: *Getting Azryah to get back with me. I've been transferred to NY for a new case and I reached out to her but she's giving me the cold shoulder.*

Me: *What can I do to help?*

Michael: *For starters, please talk to her for me. Convince her to let me come see her.*

Me: *I can talk to her but I'm not sure about her coming to see you. She's quite occupied at the moment.*

Michael: *Occupied? With what?*

Azryah hadn't come back home and I had stared at the clock plenty of times to know that she wasn't coming back this late. She was with Kaylen right now, but I had the strongest feeling that she was thinking about Khian while being with his brother. The thought of her and Khian together made me sick.

Michael: With who?

Me: Some guy... his name is Kaylen. I wasn't sure if Michael knew who Kaylen was and his dominance over Brooklyn as a drug dealer.

Michael: Kaylen Walker? The drug dealer? Well that definitely confirmed that he knew who he was.

Me: Yup. That's the one.

Anyone who was really anyone in Brooklyn knew about Kaylen and his clout on the streets. They also knew not to get on the wrong side of him because it would not have a pretty outcome.

Michael: She can't be with him.

Me: Well she is so I guess you just have to accept it.

Michael: No, she can't be with him because I'm investigating him and trying to make sure that he stays in jail for a very long time.

After all my negative thoughts about Khian leaving me, I could finally see a light at the end of the tunnel.

~ *Azryah* ~

Damn, I swear every bone in my body was broken. Most places were sore to touch, sore to move. And I only had one man to blame. He had done this to me. Even though it was an uncomfortable feeling at times, it felt good knowing that Kaylen had done this to me.

"You good over there? I've let you relax enough, pull those panties down 'cause a nigga tryna get a couple more rounds."

"You can't be serious," I voiced with shock as I stared at the growing smirk on his lips. "You know how many rounds you got in last night? I need an extremely long break, Kay."

"When was the last time you had sex?" he asked, looking at me as I lay on his king-sized bed.

"Promise me you won't laugh," I muttered shamefully.

"I won't laugh," he voiced before letting out a quiet chuckle. I threw him an unimpressed look. This liar. "Alright, alright, I promise. I was just gettin' my laughs out now."

"...Six months."

"Damn, it's been that long?" he questioned me with surprise as he moved from the doorway of his bathroom and closer to his bed.

"Yeah, I've not been with anyone since my last relationship," I explained. "Sex just hasn't been on my agenda."

"I see," he responded quietly as he climbed into the empty bedside next to me. "Well, it's definitely about to be on the agenda now. You do know that, right?"

I nodded with a shy smile, looking away from him. Only to feel my chin being pulled into his direction. He lightly pecked my lips before stating, "I really enjoyed you last night."

My shy smile widened at his words. "I really enjoyed you too."

"Like, I'm being dead ass serious... you had me feelin' shit that I don't usually feel. It's just making me realize shit."

"What type of shit?"

"Just some shit that I'd rather keep to myself right now. I don't wanna rush things and I most definitely don't want you running scared again."

I playfully rolled my eyes at him before leaning back into his lips, pecking them again. "I'm not going anywhere, Kay."

"You promise?" He gave me a hard, observant stare.

"I promise," I assured him.

"Even with what I am? What I do on a regular?"

I gave him a strange look after hearing his random questions. "Kay, where is all of this coming from?"

"I just wanna know that you're not going to be affected if you start finding out more about what I do. If it was up to me, you'd never find out a damn thing, but we're in a relationship. Not everything I'm going to be able to hide from you," he announced.

"You don't need to hide anything from me," I told him sweetly. "Just feel free enough to tell me everything there is to know."

He turned his head away from me as he stared into space, deeply thinking to himself. "I don't want you running scared, Az. I don't want you hating me."

"I'm not," I promised. "I'm not going anywhere, Kaylen. I want to be with you. I admit I was scared when you pushed me but last night, we connected on a level that I haven't reached with anyone else in a long time. I want to be with you and if you think you being a drug dealer is going to change that then you're mad. I know you're dangerous, I know you kill people, but I know you have your reasons for what you do. I don't want to focus on the negative things, I just want to focus on the positive things between you and me. And if you think me finding out more about your job is going to bring out negative things then you're right, I don't need to find out."

Kaylen kept silent but decided to wrap his arms around my waist, pulling me closer to him. I remained in his arms for a few minutes, listening to his heartbeat and hearing his light breathing.

"When I'm ready, I will," he voiced.

"That's fine with me," I lovingly answered.

My feelings for him were growing deeper and deeper. They were uncontrollable too. I wasn't going to be able to stop them after today. He had me wrapped around his little finger, no matter what he did. He had me.

I decided to come honest to him about a few things in my past while lying in his arms. I brought up my reasons for becoming a stripper and my past occupation as a child care worker. I told him how much I loved working with children, how much they loved me, and how much I cherished working at my job. But my mother was another story altogether. She made it difficult for me to get out each day because she would hurl insults at me, telling me I was worthless and never gonna be shit. And that my shitty ass job was never going to take me anywhere. I would be stuck in Chicago for life. So that's why I left her, my boyfriend, and came to New York to be a stripper. I had heard of many New York dancers who had used stripping as a way to get a better life. I had been using stripping as my way to stack and to open up my own children's daycare center in the next coming years. I wanted to prove my mother wrong and show her that I wasn't worthless.

"I wanna help you," Kaylen offered gently, wiping the tiny tears that had fallen down my cheeks. "Let me help you."

"I've got to do this on my own, Kay, I don't want you paying for it. It's something I need to do by myself," I explained.

"Okay, if you don't want me helping you pay for it, then how else can I help?"

"You can start by letting me get a job."

I remembered the first time I had brought up the topic of me getting a job. Kaylen hated it. "And supporting me in getting a loan from the bank." I originally planned to stack enough money with stripping for my center but since Kaylen didn't want me doing that, getting a loan was my next option.

"How about you just borrow the money from me?"

"Kaylen..." I wasn't sure about all that.

"What?" he asked innocently. "I'm serious. You can borrow the money from me and pay it back bit by bit on your own terms."

I didn't want him to just give me the money but borrowing it from him seemed like a much better idea than just taking it. That way, I could use the profits from my center to pay him back and I wouldn't need to worry about extra interest charges.

"Okay," I agreed happily, snuggling up closer to him. "I guess that sounds like a plan."

"You know I'm always going to have your back, Az," he commented. "Have faith in me."

"I do," I whispered to him. "I do."

I still couldn't believe that Kaylen and I had had sex last night. It was out of this world and I knew that I would keep wanting more from.

Five minutes later, Kaylen had me completely naked for him, my legs wrapped around his torso, and one hand wrapped around my throat. Not too tight but not too loose either. Just the right, firm grip around my throat. His paces were just right too. Smooth, steady paces as he dived deeper into me. All I could do was passionately moan his name, enjoying his dick penetrating in and out of my pussy.

"Kay…"

My eyes locked with his, seeing the growing lust within him. Why the hell was this man so fine? I couldn't help but admire his body, tattoos that looked like a piece of art upon his flesh. He was beyond handsome. He was beautiful. Everything about him.

Groans escaped past his lips as he continued to push in and out of me, working my middle cave perfectly, while tightening his grip around my throat.

"You sound so fuckin' sexy when you moan for me," he stated in a seductive whisper, still pushing into me. My hips moved in time with his, meeting his thrusts and feeling the overwhelming pleasure that Kaylen brought me.

"Oh… shit," I loudly moaned as he lifted my thighs and placed my legs onto his shoulder.

And that's when the freaky nature of his increased drastically.

"Oh! Oh my God… Kaylen, slow down I can—"

He cut me off immediately, "Shut the fuck up about slowin' down. Take this dick."

He wasn't hesitating at this point. His thrusts got quicker and harder into my wet slit. The sounds of our skin slapping together and his ball sack hitting against me heightened.

"Fuck, Az." He pounded in and out of me even faster and the looks of intense pleasure that were sweeping across his handsome face were driving me absolutely crazy. I didn't want this moment to end at all. My hands moved from being around his neck to being on his back. I couldn't stop clawing and scratching as he pumped steadily into my pussy.

I didn't want to admit it, but Kaylen and I having sex had just made things worse. Much worse. Because my feelings for him were growing stronger. There was no denying it. But deep down I was scared.

Scared of falling in love with a drug dealer.

CHAPTER 8

~ *Azryah* ~

~ A Week Later ~

"You're wearing the color I love on you the most. You do know that, right?"

I grinned at his sweet whispers, moving my body in time with his to the soft, sultry music. I was wearing a cream, tight fitting dress that went above my knees. It shaped my body well, almost too well, which is why Kaylen couldn't keep his hands off me right now.

"And when we get home, I'm gonna open you up, lick all up and down that pu—"

I nudged him gently, hearing him chuckle. "Stop being naughty," I playfully warned him. "We're in public and your brother's right there."

"So, he's with his date and I'm with mine. No one can hear shit but you and I," he responded innocently. "If I'm being bad what you gonna do about it?"

I felt the heat between my thighs build as I thought about being intimate with Kaylen right now. I swear this man was going to be the death of me.

"'Cause when you're being bad, I know exactly what to do about it."

"Is that right?" I cockily asked, turning around to face him and wrapping my arms around his tatted neck. His hands travelled back down to my waist, sliding around my back, and reaching down the curve of my butt.

His pink tongue parted out his lips to wet his bottom lip as he stared at me with a sexy smirk.

"So what are you go—"

Slap!

"Kaylen!" I whispered in a shocked tone, feeling flustered at his hand smacking my ass. He continued to smirk before resting his head in the nook of my neck, while massaging my butt through my dress.

"I can show you better than I can tell you," he seductively voiced, kissing lightly on my skin.

"Uh-huh," I submissively answered.

Our bodies continued to sway in time to the talented voice of Sade, who the DJ was currently playing for all the couples to slow dance to. Kaylen and I had decided to have a date night out with his twin and Michelle tonight. Things had been going good between us all, drinks flowing and conversations popping. But right now, we were each on the dance floor, more focused with our partners than the whole group.

This moment with Kaylen honestly felt amazing. And as I

continued to dance with him, I just kept on thinking about the fact that I was glad that we were together. I was glad that I had someone to hold at night, someone to make love to, someone to protect me. It all felt so wonderful. So wonderful, to the point that I felt like nothing would ever tear us apart.

But I was wrong.

While continuing to dance with him, my eyes darted to the dimly lit seating area by the bar. And that's when I spotted him. Those eyes fixed upon mine, filled with jealousy and frustration, while he drank his beer. He didn't stop staring either. Even when I tried to avoid his gaze and look elsewhere, I could still feel his burning stare on me. What on earth was he doing here? Of all the nightclubs in Brooklyn, he had to be at this one? We had never crossed the same areas before. Club Onyx had been an exception because he had found me there. But right now, I wasn't sure if this was pure coincidence or something else. One thing was for certain, the look in Michael's eyes was one that told me that trouble for me, was close by.

***

"Baby, I'm getting the bath warm, I'll call you when it's ready. A'ight?"

"Yeah," I responded casually as I stared down at my vibrating phone, while sitting on the bed edge.

We had made it back from the nightclub and even though it was 2am, neither Kaylen nor I were tired. So we decided to have a bath together. While he set it up, I was left with my phone that was now chiming in with messages from Michael.

We need to talk.

Don't ignore this.

I ain't taking no for an answer, Azryah.

Call me or I pull up on you. Not sure your little boyfriend would like that now, would he?

CHAPTER 9.

~ *Azryah* ~

Kaylen: Hurry up and get back to me. Not saying that I miss you but just hurry up.

Kaylen: I miss you.

Azryah: I'll be back soon Kay, just getting the rest of my things.

Kaylen: Call me when you're done I'll come get you.

Azryah: I drove here in your truck remember? That you insisted I take.

Kaylen: That's cool but I'm still coming to get your ass. You've been gone too long.

Azryah: Kay I left you an hour ago. Damn I ain't know you were this clingy.

Kaylen: I'm not clingy. I just want my girl with me at all times.

Azryah: Awww. I love your clingy nature though baby x

Kaylen: Stop that.

Kaylen: No ones clingy. Stop getting gassed.

Azryah: So you don't want me home now then?

Kaylen: Nah I do. Chill. You're finished?

"Azryah."

Azryah: Nope cause someone's distracting me from packing quickly.

Kaylen: A'ight I'ma leave you alone for now. Just call me as soon as you're done though.

Azryah: Cool.

Kaylen: Not a second sooner.

Azryah: Yeah yeah whatever.

"Azryah," he called out to me again but I blatantly ignored him and continued texting my man.

Kaylen: Az. Quit playing.

I sent him the eye roll emoji followed by the tongue one, teasing him further.

Kaylen: Yeah I better see that tongue in action when you get back to me.

"Azryah, I'm talking to you. Are you deaf?"

I looked up at Michael with disgust before sending one last text to Kaylen.

Azryah: Maybe if you're lucky xx

Then I locked off my phone and decided that it was time to get this over and done with. I no longer wanted anything to do with Michael but he had been the one so desperate to see me.

"You said we needed to talk when clearly, you're the one that needs to talk to me," I informed him. "Say what you need to say and make it quick, I've got stuff to do."

Today, I was going to start searching for available buildings to purchase so that I could start up my child care center. Kaylen had already loaned me the money and that meant that I was good to go with starting. I had a ton of things to do before actually buying a building but I was just so excited that I wanted to search early.

"Azryah, why are you with that psyc—"

I cut him off instantly, "Don't disrespect my man like that. If this is about him then save it. I really don't wanna hear it."

"Oh yes you do," he stated with a stern look. "He's the reason I'm here in Brooklyn."

I wasn't liking the sound of where this conversation was heading at all.

"Why is he the reason?"

"Because he's a criminal, Azryah, and you know that. Why you're with him, I'm truly confused about. I'm investigating him and his narcotics set up, that's why I got moved to Brooklyn," Michael explained firmly. "You're in a relationship with a highly dangerous drug dealer. You do know that, right?"

"It's none of your business," I mumbled, avoiding eye contact with him.

"It most definitely is if it means you could most likely go to jail alongside with him."

"What? Why? I haven't done anything."

"You're his girlfriend, which means you must know something about his operations. You're probably part of his whole set up."

"I'm not," I retorted. "Michael, you need to g—"

"Just break up with him and I promise you that you won't have no problems," Michael announced in a calm tone, making me feel very uneasy.

"Break up with him?"

"Yes, break up with him and just come back to me, Azryah. Forget about him. I know deep down you don't really like him, he probably forced you to get with him. That's how they all are, controlling and intimidating," he voiced. "He's gonna end up in jail, you don't need to worry about him coming after you. All you need to do is get back with me."

"Have you lost your mind, Michael? I'm never getting back with you and I'm not leaving him for you. I'm not leaving him at all. I like him a lot, regardless of what he does. I care about him and he cares about me. We're happy and I don't need you trying to ruin that at all. And you say you're investigating him but he's not in jail yet, he's not been arrested. Clearly, you have no evidence to charge him with."

"I don't have any evidence, yet, but I'm about to get some," he commented proudly.

"Yeah, good luck with that," I stated in disapproval.

"No, I'm not the one that's gonna need the luck," Michael announced as he moved from standing against my bedroom wall to standing in the center of my room. "You are."

"And why is that?" I asked him in a bored tone as I zipped my Nike gym bag that contained the last remaining pieces of my clothing that I needed. I had been staying so much with Kaylen that it made no sense for my stuff to be over in my apartment, so Kaylen insisted that I just move most of my stuff in with his. I wasn't permanently moving out of my apartment with Michelle but I was definitely slowly moving in with Kaylen.

"Because you're going to help me get Kaylen Walker into jail."

I let out a loud laugh at his words. A laugh that had started off short but quickly built up into an endless sound of hysterical laughter.

"I don't know why you're laughing because I'm not joking," he snapped with a frown.

I continued to laugh at him, watching him grow frustrated with me. He had to be out of his damn mind.

"I'm not doing that," I laughed. "You've lost your mind. I'm not helping you set up my boyfriend just so you can crack a case. Do that shit by yourself, you seem to be doing a great job so far that Kaylen is living his life carefree, with me."

"Well, Azryah, I just think it's funny how quickly you tend to forget about the past," Michael responded in a relaxed tone, while stepping closer to where I stood by my bedside. By now, he had pulled out his iPhone and was searching through it while walking up to me. "Let me show you something to help you remember."

"What are you tal..." My words trailed off when my eyes landed on his bright phone screen that he had now turned in my direction so

I could look at it clearly and carefully. My heart sank as I watched the video play out on the screen in front of me. My palms got sweaty and my skin felt hot as I observed the naked female in the video.

"Damn, baby, you suck this dick so good, fuck..."

I couldn't even believe that he still had this shit. And the more I stared at it, the more I quickly realized what his agenda was. This was his only play and he was going to use it to his best abilities. This bastard.

"So what? You have a video of me sucking you off, that's old news," I said, trying to play it off and not let him see that he had gotten under my skin.

"C'mon, Azryah," he gladly sang as he pulled his phone back into his direction and began scrolling through it again. "You and I both know that I don't just have one video of you."

Then he showed me another one. One of us actually fucking. Then another one of us having a threesome with some random chick he had brought along one night. Then he just kept on scrolling, showing me the collection he had of me. It seemed to run endlessly, a whole vast collection of videos I had let him record when we were together. Remember when I said we had always been one freaky couple, this is what I had meant. But a bunch of videos didn't mean shit to me and he knew that. So he had to hit me somewhere deep, somewhere too personal.

"See, not only will I send these to Kayle—"

"Send them. I don't care."

He smirked before continuing, "I'll send them to him, don't you worry, sweetheart. But I'm also going to send them to those in charge of handing out child care certificates, making sure that you're deemed as unfit to open up your center. Yeah, you ain't think I'll know about all that did you? Well guess what, I do. Now see if you don't help me, I'll make sure all these videos get sent to where they're not supposed to and ensure you don't open up your center. How that sound?" The evil look in his eyes made me want to fuck him up but I knew better. He was stronger and taller than me.

I had come so far so quickly to start building my dreams. And here stood the devil, determined to take it all away from me. I couldn't, not open my center. It meant everything to me. It was the only thing that I strived for. It was too important to me.

But Kaylen was important to me too. I didn't care about his profession. Never had and never would. I just cared about him and making sure that he was okay. I couldn't betray him. I never would. My feelings for him were too deep. But this was a conflict of interest. My center had been deep rooted in my heart long before meeting Kaylen.

"I'ma also make sure that all these videos go up on online and I'ma make a killing out of th—"

"Okay, fine! Fine! Fine!" I yelled. "I'll help you set him up."

He threw me a strange, yet surprised look. "You'll help me set him up? So that he's in jail for the rest of his life."

"…Yes," I reluctantly confirmed. "I'll help you."

~ *Kaylen* ~

"So you gon' leave her ass?" I curiously asked my brother, keeping my phone close to my ear as I rested against my leather car seat. Khian was currently filling me in on his situation with Michelle. She wanted a relationship him with him but he did not.

"Yeah," he confirmed simply. "In a few weeks."

"A few weeks?" I queried in a surprised tone. "Nigga, you said it for yourself, you weren't serious about her, so why not end all this shit now?"

"I gotta let her down bit by bit. I don't wanna hurt her feelings."

"Well damn," I commented. "I ain't know you were that nice."

"I've always been the nicer one out of both of us. You're just a savage when it comes to chicks. We both know that."

"Shit's different for me now that I have Azryah," I reminded him.

"How's things between you two?"

"They good," I told him happily. "We're gettin' to know each other much more, enjoying each other's company, and she spends almost every single night in my arms."

"That's great to hear, bro," Khian said in a pleased tone. "Just don't ruin shit between you two again. I don't wanna hear you crying like a pussy 'cause you fucked up again."

"Chill out, nigga, I won't fuck up. I'm really falling for her, so there's really no space to fuck up. She means so much to me."

Azryah was the future mother of my kids and my future wife. I could see that shit coming all down the line in the next five years. Because of her, I hadn't messed around with no other bitches. She was the only person that I had remained faithful too and I loved it. I loved the fact that we were in a committed relationship, with no drama. Everything was going so well for us and I needed it to stay like this.

"Again, that's great to hear. I'm here for your relationship with her because it's making you happy and completely sprung over her."

"Sprung?" I scoffed. "Nah, I just really like her." Deep down, I knew my brother was completely right. I was definitely sprung over Azryah.

"Whatever helps you sleep at night, bro," Khian stated amusingly. "What are your plans for today?"

"Work as per usual. What else I got planned?"

"I don't know... unless you spending the day with Azryah."

"She's out running errands and shit. Remember how I told you about her wantin' to open her own childcare center?" I questioned him, hoping he remembered.

"Yeah, yeah, I remember."

"She's just sortin' all that shit out, trying to get her certificate, and find a location."

"All sounds good. I'm happy she's doing what she loves and I'm happy you're there to help her."

All I could do was smile at my brother's words, glad that he was happy for both Azryah and me. He had always been so supportive to me, through the good and the bad. I would always appreciate him for that too.

Once I was done talking to him on the phone, I decided to get out my car and go grab some food before heading to one of my dope spots. Popeyes was the only thing that I was craving right now, so I knew I needed to have it.

When arriving into Popeyes, I joined the shortest line and waited patiently for my turn to order. It was only five minutes after staring at the food menu on the plasma screens ahead, that my eyes drifted to the female who had gotten her food.

"Serayah?"

My heart began to pound heavily as I stared at her pretty hazel eyes widening with shock. She hadn't noticed me at first but now that I had called out her name, she had recognized me without a doubt.

"Kaylen?"

Serayah Jones. The only girl that I had ever loved. The girl that had been my high school sweetheart. My best friend. But when I dropped out of high school and got arrested, we lost contact with each other.

Even after all these years, she still looked beautiful. Too fucking beautiful. Her butter pecan skin was glowing. Those pink lips were full and shaped perfectly. And why the fuck did they look so juicy and kissable? She was wearing a baby blue play suit that showcased those thick thighs of hers. She had put on weight since I had last laid eyes on her and my God... it suited her so well. She was no longer skinny and I was loving everything about her curvy figure right now. *Fuck.*

She immediately raced into my arms with joy and I found myself keeping her locked in my arms. I didn't give a shit about who was watching us right now. I had missed her ass way too much. I could never forget her because she had me feeling things that I had never felt before, until I had met Azryah. Remembering that I was in a relationship with Azryah, made me break the tight embrace I was in with Serayah. I told her to grab a seat for us, while I quickly ordered my food. Once I had my food, I went to where she had picked out and sat in front of her.

"I can't believe this is really you right now," she announced in a tone that was happy but still filled with shock.

"I can't believe this is really you too, baby girl," I responded coolly. "We've been in the same city for years and never crossed paths with each other."

"Actually, after high school, I decided to move to Canada," she explained. "I've been there ever since, I just came back from time to time to spend time with my mom."

"Well damn, that explains why we never saw each other again."

"How you've been though?" she queried, dipping a few fries into her ketchup and eating it. I remembered how we would always eat together back in the day. She had never had an issue with eating in front of me. I could clearly see that nothing had changed.

"I've been good."

"Not been getting into any trouble?"

I gave her a cheeky smile before eating into my drumstick. I knew she knew what I had become. The last day I spoke to her, I told her that

I would be dropping out of high school and becoming a drug dealer. First, she believed that I was joking, but when she saw the serious look in my eyes, she knew there was no way that I was joking.

"Kay... you could have done so much more. You were so smart, getting good gr—"

"Yeah, but that shit was never going to make me happy or become a better man," I told her, defending myself. "I'm doing something that I love."

"You love selling drugs to people?" she said in a hushed tone loud enough for my ears only.

"No, but I love making money," I answered boldly. "That's just it."

"So you don't care about all the lives you're destroying?"

"That's on them, not me. I ain't forcing anyone to buy my shit."

"But peop—"

"Serayah, stop," I cut her off, annoyed at the turn our conversation had taken. What was supposed to be a great reunion moment between the both of us, had now turned into an interrogation. "I haven't seen your ass in years and this is what you choose to speak to me about?"

She kept silent at my words and looked down at her food. I didn't want to have a conversation about my career with Azryah, so I damn sure didn't want to have a conversation with Serayah.

"You're right," she piped up. "I'm just really glad to see you."

"I'm really glad to see you too," I replied. "So... tell me how's your life in Canada been?"

***

Speaking to Serayah had been a breath of fresh air and I didn't want to stop talking to her but a nigga had work to do. We exchanged numbers though, which meant I was never losing contact with her again. She had been a very important person in my life all those years ago and I was glad that if I wanted to speak to her anytime, I could just call her. I would be lying if I said that I didn't have any feelings for Serayah, because I did. However, they weren't as strong as the feelings that I had for Azryah. Azryah was really the only priority in my life right now.

Ding!

I smiled at the text notification that had appeared on my phone screen.

I miss you.

Since I was driving, I had to dial her number quickly and put my phone on loudspeaker. She picked up on the first ring.

"Hey, baby."

"So you miss a nigga, huh?" I cockily asked. "Even though you saw me this morning and I broke that back out how many times?"

"Yeah," she laughed. "When are you coming home?"

"As soon as I'm done working."

"Which is?"

"Late, bae," I stated coolly. "Don't wait up for me."

"I want you home now though, Kay."

"And I'll be home soon, woman, shit I know you want this dick right now but relax," I amusingly voiced. "Promise I'll make it up to your pretty ass all night."

"Alright, daddy."

"Uh-uh, don't start calling a nigga that, Az, you gon' make me turn this car around to be with you."

"Then maybe you should do that."

"You know I can't, I gotta work. So shut the fuck up."

She huffed with sadness and all I could do was chuckle at her. "You run all the errands you need to, baby?"

"Yeah, most of them, but not all... I still need to go pick up some things from my apartment and I still haven't found a location I like."

"Don't sweat about it, bae, you'll find one soon enough. What about your training and certificate? You workin' on that, right?"

"Yeah... I am." I could sense some hesitation in her voice.

"Yo, Az."

"Yeah?"

"What's up?"

"Nothing," she affirmed.

"Are you sure?"

"I'm fine, Kay! Promise."

"A'ight. I need to get off the phone now, but I'll hit you up when I'm done. A'ight?"

"Okay, baby."

"I'ma see you soon."

I ended the call, locking my iPhone before stopping my car engine. A new shipment was coming in today from my connect and I needed to make sure that everything went smoothly. There could be no mistakes because I really wasn't in the mood for it. My personal life was fine, and so was my business life. I needed it to stay like that for a very long time.

"Yo, Boogie, everything good?"

"Yeah, boss. We've got half of the shipment here already, just waiting on the rest," he announced.

"Great."

Since I had taken Jermaine's territory, I now had Brooklyn under my thumb. But with that power, came more responsibility and more rivals. I had to remain alert and just make sure that no one tried me. Because I really wasn't about to let anyone cross me and think they were going to stay breathing.

CHAPTER 10

~ *Michelle* ~

As I watched him sleep, all I could think about was whether I could bear to see him with Azryah. I knew I couldn't. So should I just kill him and then kill myself so we end up in heaven together? That sounded like a decent idea but I wouldn't be happy knowing that I wasn't the mother of his children.

I was just going to have to do everything in my power to make sure that he stayed with me. I wasn't losing him to anybody and most definitely not that bitch, Azryah.

The boy is mine.

Now that I had a solid plan in action, it was only a matter of time when Azryah's happiness would come crashing down around her. Call me whatever you want. I had always been envious of her. Ever since high school. She had a great body, great chocolate skin, and niggas always lusted after her. She was earning plenty moola when at Club Onyx and that made me even more jealous of her.

Niggas wanted her and shit, bitches wanted her too. I hated to see her win in high school, now I hated to see her win at life in general. Us becoming "best friends" had always been fake. When she moved to Chicago, I was pissed that I couldn't keep a closer eye on her but then she hit me up and told me she was moving.

Only God knows how happy I felt. I could keep a closer eye on her, and if she tried anything fishy, I would ruin her. By giving Khian attention and making him like her, she had definitely done something fishy. I was going to ruin her completely. That would be the only thing to make me happy right now.

Azryah Jones completely ruined.

~ *Khian* ~

11:45am.

My eyes focused on the purple clock hung on the beige wall. What the hell was I doing?

I looked down at the covers only to be reminded that I was completely naked. Even though I told myself I was going to focus on distancing myself away from Michelle, here I was in her bed. Butt ass naked. What the fuck was wrong me? To make matters worse, she was the one that drove me here. I didn't want to take an Uber home, so I chose the next best thing.

Yo bro, come get me. Like now. Crashed at Michelle's with no car.

Within ten minutes, the fool decided to finally reply.

Why don't your dumb ass just ask her?

Khian: *Nigga this really isn't up for discussion. Come get me.*

I was annoyed and wasn't in the mood for Kaylen's games right now.

Kaylen: *You lucky that I'm in the area right now and Azryah's got some stuff remaining over there so I'm only coming to pick them up for her. You just lucky enough to hop in for a ride.*

Me: *Nigga shut up and come get me. Yo, I'm dead ass gon' fuck you up when I see you too.*

He sent me the middle finger emoji and I locked off my iPhone before heading to take a shower and freshen up. I figured Michelle was in her living room or kitchen, but at this moment, I didn't really care. All I needed was for my ass to get in the shower and change.

The warm water hitting my skin was soothing. It allowed me to be at peace with myself. The only thing I could think about right now was breaking up with Michelle. Yes, the sex was good, but I couldn't do this shit anymore. I didn't see a future with her. The main goal would be for me to end things between us.

I was wasting vital time breaking her back every single night, when I could focus on other things. Like finding a girl that I had a genuine interest in. I admit, I led her along a while but there was no more of that. It was time to be true to myself and mostly true to her. Michelle had gotten the wrong idea from the jump and I had allowed it to happen. There was no future between us, and the quicker she realized that, the better.

After my shower, I dried off, creamed my body, and got dressed. It wasn't until I entered the living room that I realized that Kaylen had arrived. He was seated on Michelle's brown loveseat with a scowl on his face. A very nasty one, I might add.

"Kaylen, what's up?"

Instead of Kaylen speaking up, Michelle who had been sitting next to him decided to speak up for him.

"He's just found out about Azryah being nothing but a snake."

"A snake? What does that mean?"

Michelle started tapping on her phone screen as she got up to walk towards me. Then, she turned her phone so I could see it while she pressed play on a voice note.

"So what? You have a video of me sucking you off, that's old news." That definitely sounded like Azryah.

"C'mon, Azryah. You and I both know I don't just have one video of you."

For a few minutes, all I could hear were moans and groans and I looked at Michelle who remained emotionless. What the hell was this?

"See, not only will I send these to Kayle—"

"Send them, I don't care."

"I'll send them to him; don't you worry, sweetheart. But I'm also going to send them to those in charge of handing out childcare certificates, making sure that you're deemed as unfit to open up your center. Yeah, you ain't think I'll know about all that did you? Well, guess what, I do. Now see if you don't help me, I'll make sure all these videos get sent to where they're not supposed to and make ensure you don't open up your center. How that sound?"

"I'ma also make sure that all these videos go up on online and I'ma make a killing out of th—"

"Okay, fine! Fine! Fine!" Azryah suddenly yelled. *"I'll help you set him up."*

You'll help me set him up? So that he's in jail for the rest of his life."

"...Yes," she confirmed. *"I'll help you."*

I really couldn't believe this shit right now. If Azryah was being blackmailed, why couldn't she have told Kaylen? And why did she agree to set Kaylen up? But why on earth did Michelle have this shit on her phone? That was the real question I wanted answers to.

"Michelle why is this on your phone?" I suspiciously asked.

"I overheard their conversation when she brought him 'round here one day. I have your best interests at heart, Khian, and I know your twin means so much to you. This conversation led to them fucking afterwards," she voiced.

"They fucked?" Kaylen suddenly spoke up, getting out his seat. "You didn't say all that!"

"I didn't say a lot of things, Kay," she told him. "That's not even the best bit."

"The best bit?" I asked in an irritated tone. Michelle and Azryah were supposed to be best friends. I didn't get why she was throwing her "best friend" under the bus.

"Yes," she said. "He's a cop."

"What?" I was appalled at this point, but still confused. Why would Azryah do this, when she's aware of what type of man Kaylen is? Fuck around with him and sooner or later, you end up missing. Speaking of Kaylen, his eyes remained frozen and fixed on Michelle. But he wasn't bothering to say a word. And that shit really scared me more than anything.

"How do you know all of this, Michelle?"

"Because Michael, the cop, is her ex-boyfriend who is investigating Kaylen. That's why he asked her to set up Kaylen. He's trying to send Ka—"

Before Michelle could finish her sentence, the front door opened and the one person I wasn't expecting walked into the apartment. Everything happened within a matter of seconds.

Kaylen lifted his shirt up and reached for his silver 9mm, loaded it, and pointed it straight at Azryah, who now looked petrified.

"Ka—"

"I swear on everything I love, I'm going to kill your dumb ass. I warned you once not to fuck with me. Now you sniffing around with cops? I fuckin' warned you and yo—"

"Kay, please calm d—" I tried to intervene but it was no use. His eyes were teary and angry. It was too late.

"No! I'm gonna kill this stupid bitch."

"Kaylen, no; please, I can ex—"

Bang!

TO BE CONTINUED

BY MISS JENESEQUA
#TheFreakInTheBooks

Lustful Desires: Secrets, Sex & Lies

Sex Ain't Better Than Love 1 & 2

Luvin' Your Man: Tales of A Side Chick

Down for My Baller 1 & 2

Bad for My Thug 1 & 2 & 3

Addicted to My Thug 1 & 2 & 3

Love Me Some You

The Thug & The Kingpin's Daughter 1 & 2

Loving My Miami Boss 1 & 2 & 3

Crazy Over You: The Love of A Carter Boss 1 & 2

Giving All My Love To A Brooklyn Street King 1

www.missjenesequa.com

Miss Jen's readers group:
https://www.facebook.com/groups/missjensreaders/

Looking for a publishing home?

Royalty Publishing House, Where the Royals reside, is accepting submissions for writers in the urban fiction genre. If you're interested, submit the first 3-4 chapters with your synopsis to submissions@royaltypublishinghouse.com.

Check out our website for more information: www.royaltypublishinghouse.com.

Text ROYALTY to 42828 to join our mailing list!

To submit a manuscript for our review, email us at
submissions@royaltypublishinghouse.com

Text RPHCHRISTIAN to 22828 for our
CHRISTIAN ROMANCE novels!

Text RPHROMANCE to 22828 for our
INTERRACIAL ROMANCE novels!

Do You Like CELEBRITY GOSSIP?

Check Out QUEEN DYNASTY!
Visit Our Site: www.thequeendynasty.com

Get LiT!

Download the LiTeReader app today and enjoy exclusive content, free books, and more

CPSIA information can be obtained
at www.ICGtesting.com
Printed in the USA
LVOW08s2051070817
544137LV00021B/562/P